MUMFORD "88"

VANESSA B. JACKSON

Mumford "88"

When things fall apart — they fall apart so hard — and when things come together — they come together so well.

Namaste ⚖

Summer 1988

To Liz
Jad
V...
10-2-71

Mumford "88"

Table of Contents

- Chapter 1 – Penn's Landing   6
- Chapter 2 – Show Down   12
- Chapter 3 – Summer Solstice   17
- Chapter 4 – Spa Day   22
- Chapter 5 – The Discovery   27
- Chapter 6 – Aftermath   30
- Chapter 7 – The Investigation   33
- Chapter 8 – The Arrest   36
- Chapter 9 – Come to Terms   39
- Chapter 10 – All in the Family   43
- Chapter 11 – The Restaurant   47
- Chapter 12 – The Trial Begins   52
- Chapter 13 – Hello College   57
- Chapter 14 – The Night   61
- Chapter 15 – All Grown Up   69
- Chapter 16 – Not Easy   72
- Chapter 17 – Graduation   77
- Chapter 18 – The Party   88

Mumford "88"

- *Chapter 19 – Student Leader*   91
- *Chapter 20 – Revelation*   98
- *Chapter 21 – The Wedding*   101
- *Chapter 22 – The Reception*   109
- *Chapter 23 – Conclusion*   118
- *Note to self: Soul Mate —*   121
- *Guided Mindfulness Scripts –*   122
- *Note to self —*   124

Editor: Rayyonia N. Jackson

Mumford "88"

Chapter 1: Penn's Landing

School is out for the summer, and two teenage athletes are gearing up for what could be their most compelling summer ever.

She's happy, energetic, and full of life—her name is Tray—and she loves the summer months. It was summer 1988, and Tray was super excited because her team recently ranked one of the top groups in the Penn Relay—Girls 4x800-meters race. The event is for track & field athletes—the teams consist of four runners—each complete an 800-meter run or two laps on a standard 400-meter field. Tray enjoys sprint training—but she also enjoys long-distance running—it appears she could practice for hours. Indeed, long-distance running requires endurance, stamina, and mental strength. The question of the day is—is Tray a soul running for endurance, or is she running from something? Does she constantly keep herself busy with track practice because she is trying to escape adversities and hardships in her personal life? We will soon discover the motive behind Tray's fortitude. Here's how the story goes.

Mumford "88"

Come on, Janey, let's get ready to exercise; you know you must be in shape if you want to make the track team our senior year of high school.

Girl, I don't want to run track for Mumford High or any other school that is. I run for fun, for exercises, for energy, for a boosted immunity—and most importantly, for a fit physique and a healthy body. *Janey followed her statement with a little dance.*

Ha-Ha, you're hilarious, Janey, but on the real, I think you should try out for the team, you're athletic—and you're almost as fast as me on the field.

Naw, Tray, that's not for me, that's your thing. As a matter of fact, it appears that lately you've been focused on running and exercising more than normal—you're obsessing, and now you're trying to get me to join your madness. Tray you are always on the go, always ready to run-run-run; you have practice on the mind 24-7...

Yes, I do, Tray said eagerly—and so do you, Janey. Don't act like just last week you weren't trying to get me to go running in the middle of a rainstorm.

Girl, it was a few drizzles, and besides, the rain feels good when working up a sweat.

Oh really, Janey? Now who sounds like a fanatic?

We both are fanatical, Janey alleged.

Um, maybe we are, I'm not going to argue with you on that—okay, stretching time is over, I'm ready to feel the pavement on my feet and the wind in my hair, let's go, Janey. *The girls' jog to Penn's landing with eagerness, happiness, and fulfillment.*

Destination Penn's Landing. Woohoo! We did it, Janey—that was an amazing run, and it will break our long-distance record when we jog back home later this evening.

Yes, girl, we are breaking records left and right; but before we jog back home and rack up those miles, we must rest, I'm exhausted as hell.

I'm okay with that, Tray agreed; I'm fatigued too, and I need a moment just to enjoy the scenery and unwind. Lately, I've been meditating and practicing breathing techniques after strenuous workouts; let's give it a try, Janey, I'm sure you will like it. Just relax and focus on your breathing; listen to the sounds of our environment, smell the fresh air, become one with the location, become one with self.

Mumford "88"

Okay, Tray. I'll give it a try—it sounds soothing and relaxing, let's do it, Janey said excitedly. Janey, maybe you can discover your calm within as you sit in a comfortable position and, if possible, try focusing on the now. Find comfort and peace as you concentrate on your breathing. Feel the air on your face, listen to the sounds of the Delaware River, hear the people talking and laughing from afar—as you inhale and exhale, breathing in positivity and exhaling negativity. Maybe you can take a deep breath in and hold it for a few seconds before exhaling. Perhaps you can visualize the oxygen nourishing your internal organs—and envision toxicity exiting your body through your nostrils or mouth. Finding ways to rid our bodies of harmful thoughts, feeling, emotions, or in our case at this present moment, an intense jog/run truly is priceless... *Tray speaks in a subtle and relaxed tone as Janey listens and complies with ease.*

A few moments later. Namaste, Janey, relaxation time is over—my intuition tells me to share something very personal and private with you. I must get this issue off my chest; I cannot keep the secret any longer; it's eating me up inside.
Talk to me, Tray, what's going on, girl; are you okay? You're making me nervous.
Yes, I'm okay, or I will be—once I complete my senior year of high school and head to college. I cannot take living at home anymore; the energy is very tense around my house.
Tense, what do you mean tense? Is your mom beating on you or making you do insane chores around the house or something like that?
No, it's nothing like that.
Then tell me what's going on, you're scaring me, Tray. Please, talk to me, stop beating around the bush, the suspense is driving me insane, you know I have little patience, what's up, girl?
Okay, you know how my mom finally got a boyfriend?
Yeah, I remember you were so happy when Ms. Ava found someone she truly cared for.
Well, that ship has sailed, Janey. I was once joyful, but now, I'm not. John from San Diego is always at my house, and my mom just informed me that he would be moving in with us once his lease is up on his apartment next month. As you know, John was in town on business when he met my mother. As a result, he decided to stay in Philadelphia and find employment on the East Coast—John adjusts insurance claims for major hospitals and dental practices.
Yeah-Yeah, I know what he does for a living, so, what's the issue, girl?

Mumford "88"

The problem is that my mom's man has a touching problem; he cannot keep his hands to himself if you know what I mean?

No, I do not know what you mean, please elaborate more, Tray; I don't want to jump to conclusions here.

Breathe Tray, Breathe, *Tray mumbles to herself as she searches for the right words to start the conversation.*

Okay, so about six months ago, my mom was at work, and my little sister Beverly was fast asleep. I was in the kitchen, studying when John came in to get a glass of water. He sat down next to me and asked me what I was working on, I told him a science project, and he was willing to help with the research. I was grateful; John had a profound understanding of the project I was working on. This went on for about three weeks; he made a habit of helping me with my homework—I felt like I had a personal tutor, it was very nice.

But one evening when my mom went out to have a few drinks with her girlfriends, John came into my bedroom and asked me a question, I'm not sure what he asked because I felt uneasy and frightened—as I was unsure why he would come into my bedroom. The next thing I knew, he got into my bed, and when I tried to get up, he grabbed me by my hair and slammed me back on the bed. He proceeded to get on top of me, to which I yelled—then he put a cloth or something over my face; I think it was saturated with chloroform because the next thing I remember was waking up with my nightgown over my head, and my body felt strange. I was confused and in a lot of pain; I laid in my bed all night, afraid to move once I regained consciousness. Later that night, when my mother came home, I heard her and John talking about her night out on the town. They were laughing, having a good time, which further deepened my daze—I think I was in shock.

I gazed out my bedroom window, looking at the stars all night, I was unable to fall to sleep, but finally, as daybreak was approaching, I drifted into dreamland. The next morning when I was sleeping, my mom took my sister to my grandmother's house, and John and I were home alone. He came back into my bedroom to tell me that if I tell anybody, he would deny it—and then he proceeded to say, "who do you think your mother will believe, a little whore like yourself or me?" I went buck-wild on him, then he threw me to the floor and told me to knock it off. He made threats against my little sister and said he would hurt my mother if I ever told anybody. I was so frightened. Thankfully, I don't remember him actually molesting me because I was unconscious as a result of the chloroform. Still, I'm sure he penetrated me, because of the pain I felt when I awakened.

Hold up, hold the fuck up, right now! Hell No, I'm calling the police, Janey shouted loudly. *Tray jumped up and told Janey to keep her voice down.* The incident happened over three months ago, and he hasn't tried anything since then.
I don't give a damn how long it has been since he sexually assaulted you; John must pay for what he did to you, that perverted motherfucker is going to get what he deserves. If you do not want me to call the cops, please let me call my brother Derek—he has a few friends who will fuck John's punk-ass up. They will make John wish he never stepped foot on the East Coast.

Janey, I said no! Darn. Don't cause any trouble for my mother and me, keep your mouth shut.
Look, Tray, you have a choice, I can call my brother Derek—or I can call the cops, it's your decision—a payphone is only a few feet away, the choice is yours. So, what's it going to be?
Okay. Darn, Janey, you always get so worked up, call Derek.
Ring-Ring-Ring...
Hello, who is this, Derek ask with curiosity because he doesn't recognize the phone number.
Derek, this is Janey; I need your help. I need you to come and get me—right now. I'm at Penn's Landing with Tray!
Hey, little sis, what's up—and why are you yelling? *Janey continued screaming and hollering in her brother's ear, trying to tell him the story in a nutshell. Finally, Derek gets a word in and says, "Who did what now?" Janey started over and informed Derek that Tray's mother's new boyfriend, John, molested and drugged Tray a few months ago—and she concluded with,* "And I'm just finding out about it today—so what the fuck are we going to do about it?"
Say no more, Janey—which part of Penn's landing are you at; I'm coming for you and Tray?
Janey gives her brother the location, and he rushes there to pick them up.

Janey, I should have never told you, my mother is going to be so upset with me.
Forget your mother, your what matters here, not your mother's feelings about a man she barely knows—and had the audacity to move in with her minor children. Sorry, but I'm pissed—and Tray, *you* have a right to be upset too—*you* have a right to tell people what happened to you,

Mumford "88"

especially your mother and the police. You shouldn't be afraid of John and his idle threats. I wish you would have told me sooner, but I'm happy you told me today. Now I understand why you and your little sister Beverly have been staying at my house almost every night.

Yes, I'm trying to protect her, if John did that to me—there's no telling what he will try to do to Bev. She's so young and innocent.

John's a dead man if he tries anything with her, I guarantee you that! Oh great, here is my brother now; come on, girl, let's go!

Chapter 2: Show-Down

Derek, you got here fast, you must have been speeding. You're lucky the cops didn't pull your butt over, aren't you tired of getting traffic tickets? *Derek ignored his sister's smart remark; he knows she always has something slick to say.*

Janey, your brother drove us here like a mad man; he didn't say one word, just, "lets Rock & Roll, my sister needs me." So please, tell us what the fuck is going on? *Janey and Tray got into the car, and Tray explains the situation and closes with,* "but I don't want any trouble, also I don't want anybody going to jail over me, so please don't do anything crazy." *Derek interrupts Tray with an angry tone;* We are like family and family must get into trouble when it comes to helping their loved ones. There is no way in the fucking world we are going to let that fool get away with that shit!

Please don't kill him, Derek, please, Tray utters. I don't want anyone murdered because of me. I promise you we won't kill that bastard, but punk-ass John will get the beatdown of his life, I promise you that!

Mumford "88"

A few minutes later. Okay, ladies, go inside the house and get cleaned up, I cannot believe you guys jogged to Penn's Landing, but that's what's up, you girls are getting stronger and faster by the day. Janey, look after your friend, and we will talk later this evening.

Okay, bro, be safe and don't do anything too crazy, you know mom will have a heart attack if something happens to you or me.

I'll be safe sis, don't you worry about me.

The girls are at Derek and Janey's house (their mom's house shall I say), trying their best not to think about what Derek might do once he finds John.

Tray, you shower first and take all the time you need. I'll make us a Greek salad, and some fresh-squeezed lemonade. How does that sound?

Okay, that sounds good to me—but instead of lemonade, can you make that tequila? Girl, I need a few shots right about now, I'm nervous as fuck!

Sure, Tray. Derek has an alcohol stash in his room; I just have to find it. Tequila, it is!

****

Later that evening. Hey, Janey, where is Beverly and your sister Kimmy, are they still at that birthday party on the other side of town with your mother?

Yeah, they are, they should be home around 8 p.m., my mother called when you were in the shower, she said everything was going well, and the girls are having a great time.

Okay, cool, that gives us time to relax and have a few shots of Tequila. The shower was relaxing, but I'm still nervous about what Derek will do once he finds John.

Everything will be okay, you know Derek will handle the situation properly, let's wait to see what happened when my brother returns, but I doubt he'll be home anytime soon—so let's focus on something else. *Tray and Janey have a few shots and discuss college life. Janey wanted to distract Tray from thinking about the current situation. The discussion about college, along with alcohol, did the trick—and for the first time in a long time, Tray's mind was free and clear.*

A few hours later. Hey, what's all the noise about, and what time is it? *Tray was confused—as she was waking up from a tequila induced nap, those shots knocked her out.* I must have dozed off, but I feel much better now. Who's shouting, is that Beverly and Kimmy making all that noise, are they back from the birthday party?

Girl, your waking up asking one thousand questions—we had three shots of tequila and was talking about how you cannot wait to leave for college—and why it is for you and not for me—and before I know it, you were out like a light. Kimmy and Bev are sleeping; they ate dinner at the birthday party, they came home, got cleaned up, watched a movie on the big screen TV in the basement, then fell to sleep around 11 p.m. The loud noise was Derek and his boys.

Oh, okay. So, what happened with John, Janey. Did Derek tell you how the evening went?

No, I didn't get the scoop yet. Derek will tell us in a few; he's in his bedroom at the moment—he'll be out shortly—be patient, girl!

Oh, Okay. Well, did my mother call, Tray asked.

Yes, Ava called here about forty-five minutes ago.

Ava, huh, Tray uttered.

Yes, Ava, any woman who moves a man in with her children and has a blind eye to physical and mental abuse do not get *Ms.* from me, so yes, Ava. I'm sorry Tray, I'm too upset to call her anything else at the moment, my apologies—I need time to process the information.

Understood, Janey—but it isn't my mom's fault; she's not responsible for what John did to me; she has no control over the situation.

Sure, if you say so, Tray.

So, what did my mom want, was she asking if Beverly and I were coming home tonight? No, she wasn't concerned about you or Bev, sorry. Your mom was worried about John; she wanted to know if you been to the house today and if you saw John. I told her no—we haven't seen him and informed her that we were here the entire day, minus the jog and the birthday party.

Oh, wow, okay, Tray said dreadfully.

At that moment, Derek enters the room and asks Janey and Tray to meet him in the kitchen.

Tray, you will not have any more issues with John, we kicked his ass up and down the basketball court, literally. He may have a few broken bones, but he will live, as promised.

Mumford "88"

What, are you serious, so you didn't kill him?
No, Tray, I told you I wouldn't—but if you want him gone, say the word.
No! That's okay, Derek. Thank you so much for all that you have done!
Tray, If I hear anything else about John, I guarantee you that promise *will* be broken, *then Derek turns and leaves the room.*
So, Tray, I guess your mom was concerned because John didn't make it home yet. But I guess an ass-kicking will make anybody late getting home. Street justice has been served—and John got what he deserved, well actually, he got off easy; he deserves much more than an ass-kicking—but I'm somewhat satisfied with the results, are you, Tray?
Yeah, I am Janey. I'm pleased and grateful. Thanks for helping me handle the situations, you and Derek are the best! I feel like my mind can rest—now that someone knows the truth. It felt good to talk to someone; talking really does help relieve built-up tension.
You're our sister from another mother, girl; we got you, and I'm happy your mind can find some sort of comfort and peace! And I'm happy you feel less anxiety; you've been carrying a heavy burden for months now—you're a stoic, such tolerance.
Thanks, girl—and I truly am content with the way Derek handled John; I just feel a little off because I don't know what he will tell my mother about his beatdown. But honestly, I don't care.
I'm sure John will not tell your mother the truth, Tray; he knows your mom will have him arrested, certainly. Trust, he will make up a lie, that's what he's good at.

Yeah, you're right. I'm sure he will... Anyway, I'm glad no one was murdered. I don't know if I could have lived with myself, knowing I was responsible for another person's death, that reality would have been a hard pill for me to swallow.
Well, I'm happy it didn't come to that either; there are ways to solve problems without death being the ultimate outcome. *Janey had a strange feeling when she said that statement but kept the emotion to herself. At that moment, Derek came back into the kitchen.*

Okay, ladies, I'm headed out for the evening, I'm going to one of my sortie's houses for the night. You girls have a good evening and get some sleep, try to relax. Oh, and don't think I don't realize you were in my liquor stash, but it's cool, I understand, considering the circumstances.

Janey and Tray felt relief when Derek didn't grill them for drinking alcohol at such a young age, then Janey tried to change the subject. Derek, you're leaving back out again?

Yes, Janey, I am, if you must know. I only came home to inform you that the situation has been handled, now it's time for *me* to relax. Now, remember Tray, if John tries anything ever again, make sure you call me directly, and next time it won't be just a beat down, you understand?

Yes, I do—and thanks again, Derek, Tray said graciously.

You're welcome, Tray. And I heard what you and Janey were saying a few moments ago, and you *are* like a little sister to me, and we *are* family, remember that!

Will do, Derek. I appreciate those kind words. Have a good night; see you tomorrow.

It's been 45 days since John's beatdown, and Tray is getting her life back on track. She and Beverly are no longer staying at Janey's house, and Tray is starting to feel safe at home again.

Chapter 3: Summer Solstice

Tray is on fire today; she's motivated and determined—she's also super excited about her future in track and field. Let's go, everybody; it's the Summer Marathon Track Meet—I've been training all season for this day and the Penn Relays, of course. I cannot believe I'm here. Janey, I want to thank you for being such a great friend—and for practicing with me and jogging all those miles to Penn's Landing with me, day after day—week after week. I appreciate you so much! To be here, right now, at this moment, is freaking amazing. And Janey, guess what, you're never going to believe it—I received notice that I will most likely get a full scholarship. If my academics and athletic abilities continue to improve at an accelerated rate, I'm going to college, girl; I'm on cloud nine right about now. I'm so happy I feel like I'm going to explode; oh, the excitement, my heart feels so good right about now!

Wow, I've never seen you this enthusiastic before Tray, it's a great look on you. I'm so proud of you, girl. I'm happy you are following your dreams; you are becoming everything you imagined you would be, plus so much more. I'm positive you will become a renowned track star in no time, keep moving forward, you got this!

Mumford "88"

So, you will be leaving for college come Fall 1989; you go, girl. But before you leave for school, you *must* inform your mother about the assault. If you do not tell Ms. Ava, you will be inadvertently putting your little sister at risk of suffering the same abuse you endured months ago—and I know you don't want that fate for Beverly.
Janey don't worry about it—everything has been great at home; ever since Derek and his boys handled business, John has gotten his act together! He apologized to me a thousand times and blamed his behavior on illicit drugs—he has been clean for months. Besides, I don't remember the actual assault—and I believe John when he said, "he will never hurt me ever again," trust me, he has learned his lesson.
Tray, you are as nice as they come, and sometimes very naive—be careful; a zebra doesn't change their stripes overnight. But I'm warning you—if you leave for college without telling your mother, I will tell her, I must.
Okay, Janey, darn; let up! I will handle it—when I'm ready, at my pace...
Okay! We will see... *Janey and Tray look at each other with tension and agitation.*

Listen, Janey, I know you hate John.
Yeah, your right, I do.
But please do not lose your head today.
What... why would I snap, Tray? I don't have any reason to lose my shit.
Yeah, you do. My mom, Beverly, and John are supposed to be coming to the Summer Solstice race today, to support me and to cheer me on.
Are you fucking kidding me? Do you think that's a good idea with all that has occurred? Giving the illusion of a happy family, that isn't a wise decision, Tray.
It's not an illusion Janey, I just told you things are much better; in fact, better than ever.
The quiet before the storm, Janey uttered—the quiet before the storm.
Janey, I don't want to hurt my mom; she's so happy right now, and John is good to her. It's me who has the issue with him.
I must stop you right there, Janey asserted. John is *not* good to your mother; he sexually assaulted her daughter, which indicated he is most likely cheating on your mother as well, "A good man for your mom," I don't think so. He's a pig, and if he comes here today, I will not be

anywhere near him. I will keep my distance because I *won't* be able to keep my cool—you forgave him, I did not!

Okay, but please don't make a scene—I know how you get, Janey.

I promise you—I will not cause any trouble on your special day; you have my word, but you are putting me in a shitty situation, and I didn't like it… I'm going to respect your wishes… but if John does anything rude, condescending, disrespectful, or sexist against females, I will have his head on a fucking platter, I *promise* you that!

Okay, sounds like a deal—thank you for understanding and for being a good friend.

You're welcome, Tray. Now forget about John and your mom—get warmed up for the race, you got this—it's all you, girl!

Thank you… *Tray uttered as she jumped up in down in place, getting warmed up for the event. And just like true friends, Janey and Tray had a moment of heat, but never will they allow disagreements to interfere with their friendship.*

A few moments later. Mom, over here, Tray shouted. My team is running 3rd this season, so be in your seats by 10:45 a.m., I don't want you to miss any of the action, it's going to be intense. The rival teams are really good, and I'm looking forward to the challenge!

Okay, dear, I'm excited too, break a leg, or whatever they say before a big track meet.

Thanks, mom—oh and Bev, make sure you drink plenty of water, give the soda and juice a break, on hot days like this, water is essential.

Okay, big-headed sister, you told me this when we first arrived.

Yeah, and I still don't see a water bottle in your hand. Mother, please make sure Bev gets water, not soda.

Okay, Tray, prepare for the race—I got Bev, we will see you after—love you, and have fun.

Love you too, mom. *Tray looked at John, turned, and walked away.*

Everyone shouted, "Let the games begin," as Tray took her place on the field. Fortunately, Tray heard them and waved their way and gave them two thumbs up. Tray was feeling great; she felt like her family was finally strong again—and she was happy to have her best friend cheering her on—and most importantly, she was happy to see that her mom was finally happy. The breakup between Tray's parents was horrible—her mom was unhappy for a very long time, that was until she met John.

****

After the race. You were amazing; you killed it on the field—you were looking and moving like *Flo Jo*. Whichever college you choose—they're going to be fortunate to have such an amazing athlete representing their University, Ava professed with excitement to her daughter.
They sure are, Janey agreed.
High Five, Bev said with a huge smile on her face.

Thanks, guys. Man, the sun was beating down on me, and I thought I was going to faint on the field, but I kept pushing forward until I reached the finish line, it felt amazing—I definitely leveled up after this race. And the humidity, oh my goodness, it's so hot!
Girl, who are you telling, the sun was beaming on us too—we were baking sitting on those hot ass bleachers, Janey uttered playfully.
Watch your mouth!
Oh, sorry, Ms. Ava, my bad; I forgot you were here for a second.
Hey, Janey, come here I want to talk to you in private, *Tray pulled Janey to the side.* Where did Derek and John go? I saw them walking away as I was coming over; you didn't tell Derek to beat John up again, did you?
No girl, relax. John said he had to use the bathroom, and Derek followed him!
Oh, okay, so why are you smiling, Janey?
No reason, but I'm pretty sure Derek will have a few reassuring words with John, and sometimes a pep talk is needed. Anyway, Tray, forget about that fool—let's stand and celebrate with the family*, they stepped closer to the group.* Todays about you—and you were on fire! You lit the field up; I'm so proud of you, girl, Janey proclaimed with enthusiasm.

Yeah, you were super-fast, Tray; I could have sworn I saw smoke coming from your sneakers, Beverly uttered playfully.

Mumford "88"

Bev, you have an amazing imagination—you always know exactly what to say to make me smile. *Tray hugged Bev, and started giggling; thus, everyone started cracking up laughing as they imagined smoked coming from Tray's sneakers; it was a hilarious image.*

Yes, dear, your speed *is* improving drastically, you're much faster than last year, you're growing as an athlete, I'm so proud!

Thanks, mom… thanks, everyone—I appreciate the support. I'm happy you all made it out to the event today—and on such an extremely hot day at that, you guys are the best!

We wouldn't be anyplace else, Tray's mother proclaimed; we are here for you!

Yes, we are, Janey agreed.

**** 🏆 ****

A few moments later in the restroom: Derek and his boys walked up on John—and John apologized profusely for what he had done—ensuring Derek that he was high on drugs that night, and it will never happen again. Derek warned John that "you owe your life to Tray, she begged us not to lullaby your ass. But if you ever hurt her or any female again, pow-pow, enough said."

I understand completely, John said. And I'm thankful I'm not in jail or dead; you have my word; it will *never* happen again. *Derek looked at John crudely and walked away.*

Come on, let's go, Derek said to his boys. We are not staying for the second half; I want to get out of here before the traffic gets crazy, you know how the city gets during these track and field events. *Derek makes the impression of a firearm with his fingers—points at John and says, "Pow-Pow" as he walks out the restroom. John feels relieved and simultaneously grateful that he didn't get another beat-down from Derek and his boys.*

Chapter 4: Spa Day

Tray and Janey are excited to be starting their final year of high school—classes start in less than five weeks—and Tray has one final track & field event before her senior year at Mumford High. It's an exciting time because every year, the impending senior class takes an annual hiking trip to celebrate the end of the summer and the beginning of the new and final school year—and like many Mumford High graduates, Tray and Janey are looking forward to the event.

Janey, we need to go to the spa today. I'm sore from all the intense training we put ourselves through over the summer break. I can use a massage, and heat therapy sounds good right about now. My body will benefit from the heat of a sauna and a masseuse hands on my body; I can just imagine it now. What do you think, Janey, do you want to be in heaven or not?

Okay, girl, the spa sounds good to me. Let me check my ATM balance to make sure I have enough cash; I want to get my hair and nails done too—I mean, if we are at the spa—I might as well splurge, you know?

Mumford "88"

I heard that, Janey. I wish I could get my hair and nails done also—but I leave for the final summer track meet tomorrow evening, so I cannot. But I'll treat myself to a fresh hairstyle, manicure, and pedicure when I return—God knows I'll need it. I know my roots are going to get sweated out over the weekend.

Okay, Tray, sounds like a plan—let's go to the spa and relax in the sauna and jacuzzi area. But I'm still getting my hair and nails done once we're done with our peace and tranquility session—I'm pampering myself today, girl—I need this!

At the spa. Oh, my Goodness, girl, this pedicure feels so goddamn good; it's just what I needed, self-care *is* a necessity, huh Tray?

Yes, it is, Janey. I don't know why we didn't come here earlier in the season. The décor, ambiance, and aromatherapy are so soothing—do you smell the scented oils girl, incredible; I'm so relaxed. And to top it off, they gave us a discount because we are high school students, what more can we ask for, gotta love discounts?

I know, right! I'm a satisfied consumer, Tray. And I'm at awe with the layout of this place, and their customer service *is* to die for.

A few moments later. Hey Janey, you remember Bobby from 9th street, don't you?

Yeah, girl, he's been trying to talk to me since middle school. Why, what's up?

Nothing much, but I saw him at the market yesterday evening, and he was asking me about you—he said he gave you his number *several* times, and you have yet to call him.

Yeah, girl, Bobby's persistent, but I'm focused at the moment—relationships often end with broken hearts, so I decided to wait until college before I date. I'm looking for a mature guy, someone who won't play childish games.

Hold up now, Bobby's head is on straight, and you know it, Janey. That guy is "the real deal." I think you should call him and see if there is a connection; it won't hurt to call the guy.

Okay, maybe I will. I'll think about it on the drive home—Derek is picking us up afterward.

Cool, we don't have to walk home today, oh yeah! Oh, guess what, Janey? I have some exciting news. John asked my mother to marry him last month. I wasn't going to tell you, but since we're at the spa and I'm feeling all relaxed and stuff, I figured what the heck.

Mumford "88"

Wow, okay. I think it's a bad idea, and I think your mother needs to know who she's engaged to, but I'm your friend, and I'll mind my business and keep my mouth shut because you asked me to, even though I don't agree with your silence.
Thank you, girl, I appreciate that, and I appreciate you.
I know you do, Tray—and ditto, I appreciate you too.
But honestly, Janey, I think my mom and John will be happily married; the past is the past.
Maybe they will, Tray; only the future will tell. But respectfully, I do not want to talk about John; I despise him, so please, let's change the subject.

Fair enough. So, Janey, I really hope you decide to call Bobby tonight? You're getting your hair and nails done; you might as well let him take you out—enjoy the evening, let your hair down—you deserve it, girl.
Okay, alright. I will call Bobby and maybe go out with him *if* the conversation goes well.
Sounds like a good move, I'm sure you two will have lots of things to discuss, I think you guys look great together. He really likes you, his face light up whenever he speaks about you.
Okay, Tray, you convinced me, I will call Bobby and see what he has to say, who knows, maybe it will lead to something special!
Tray and Janey had a relaxing day at the spa; they sipped on tea and listened to meditation music. Later that evening, Janey called Bobby, and they had an eventful first date.

**** ****

The next day. Ring-Ring-Ring...
Hello, Tray, It's me girl. I do not feel well; my stomach is in knots. I don't think I can drive to Maryland with you and your teammates this evening. I went to that new sushi restaurant with Bobby last night; we had an amazing time by the way—thanks, girl, for encouraging me to go out with him, but my tummy is not happy today. I cannot leave the house; I'm afraid I might shit myself if I go too far from the bathroom, I'm so sorry, Tray. But I will ask Derek to drive me to the cabin tomorrow; I'll catch the second half of the track meet—I'm sure the bug will be out of my system by then. I'll tell you one thing; that will be the last time I eat sushi ever again!

Mumford "88"

Okay, girl, feel better. I'm packing my suitcase and getting ready to head over to the recreation center—I'm looking forward to seeing you tomorrow evening, I want to hear all about your date with Bobby—but now I must finish packing.

Wait, Tray, why are you rushing me? I'm not ready to hang up the phone yet. What time is the team headed to the cabin—it's still early in the day, why are you leaving the house so soon?

Well, we're not leaving Philly until 3 p.m., but I'm going to the recreation center early because I want to be the first one there—I want a window seat on the van, girl. Also, I'm bored out of my mind, my mother and Bev already left for the shore with my aunties and all their badass kids. So, I'm ready to get out of this house and start my weekend.

Oh yeah, that's right; everyone went to the beach—that sounds like so much fun.

It sure does, but we will be hiking in the woods in three weeks, so I'm not envious, Janey.

Lol, neither am I, Janey agreed. Okay, finish packing, I have to run to the toilet, again. Shit, I have to pop girl, my intestines are in knots.

You're so crazy, bye, Janey—and love you. I will see you tomorrow when Derek brings you to Maryland; I hope you feel better—and don't forget to take the air fresher into the bathroom with you!

Ha-Ha, you got jokes, Tray, and I love you too. Adios, I must go!

Alright, Janey. I think I just heard John walk in, he's headed to New York for a wedding—his best friend from high school is having a bachelor party, so he didn't go with my mother, but I thought he left already. Let me see what's up; I will talk to you later.

Okay, Tray, I'll see you soon! *Janey hangs up the phone as she was already on the toilet pooping in agony. That sushi and her intestines were battling it out!*

John, what are you still doing here—I thought you were already in New York getting ready for the big Bachelor party weekend?

Nope, change of plans, we're going to have the bachelor party in Downtown Philly. Driving and parking are more convenient in Philadelphia. New York traffic can be heavy at times.

Okay, well I'm getting ready to go to my track and field meet, I'll be out of your way soon enough, just ack like I'm not here.

Tray was done packing and headed down the hallway when she noticed John was smoking something in her mother's room. So, Tray quietly walked down the stairs and headed out the front door. But before she reached the door, she noticed John was coming up from behind and said, "wait a sec – I have something for you." Tray stopped right before the foyer and asked, "what is it? I must go; I'm running late," John says, "you forgot your kiss." Tray looked bewildered; she turned away from John and ran for the front door. Regrettably, John was able to grab Tray from behind, preventing her from exiting the house. He threw Tray to the floor and dared her to get up.

John what are you doing, get off me, stop, your hurting me. *Tray shouted fearfully and desperately. But her screams went on deaf ears, and John continued to assault her. Tray fought back with force; kicking, biting, and screaming, she managed to get a few hits in, she even caused John's nose to bleed. But John eventually overpowered Tray; thus, punching her until she lost consciousness. And like the sexual predator that he is, John sexually assaulted Tray as she laid there helplessly. Tray started to regain consciousness, and at that moment, John put his hands around her neck, strangling her until there was no more breath left inside of her body.*

What have I done, what have I done? *John is high as a kite, as he rants to himself.* Oh my God, I must leave town now. Let me pack all my shit and get the fuck out of here! She was asking for it; she looked too good, sexy, athletic; she made me do it; it wasn't my fault. *Note, abusers never take responsibility for their actions.*

John leaves the city and heads back to San Diego via automobile. Three days have gone by, and Tray never made it to her track meet. Her mother and Janey assume Tray is safe and sound with her track coach and fellow teammates. Regrettably, the reality of the situation is far worse.

"Tray, this is the 4th message I left for you at the front desk—I'm so sorry I didn't make it to Maryland this weekend. The stomach virus I had was worse than I thought, I was rushed to the hospital later that evening. They kept me for two days—I'm home now and feeling much better, please call me back. Ps. I'm going to meet you at the recreation center; I will be there when the van arrives back in town, so you cannot stay upset with me for much longer, I'll see you soon."

Chapter 5: The Discovery

Hello, Coach Trench, how are you, and how was the Maryland track meet? Everyone looks happy and well-rested. Oh, I see the team won a few trophies, very nice!
It was great, Janey. Everyone had their game faces on and was ready to compete.
Cool. Well, where Is Tray? I think she is upset with me because I didn't make it to the track meet—I called several times, but I wasn't able to reach her.
What are you talking about, Janey? Tray never made it to the track meet this weekend. I figured her mother changed her mind and made Tray go to the shore with the family.
What. No. Tray was packing—she was getting ready for the Maryland trip the last time we spoke; her mother had already left for the shore. I'm confused, I'm not sure what's going on, but I'm going to her house, something must be wrong; this isn't like her. Tray wouldn't miss a track meet for anything in the world, and you know it, coach; she's as dedicated as they come.
Okay, Janey. Please have Tray call me once you speak with her; now I'm worried.
I will, coach Trench. I will have her call you the moment I get done cursing her out.

Mumford "88"

All sorts of thoughts are running through Janey's head as she power-walks seven blocks to Tray's house. Because Janey was sick, she didn't think anything of it—but in an instant—after realizing Tray never made it to the track meet, Janey thought of the last thing Tray said, "John just walked in, I'll talk to you later." Janey's emotions got the best of her; thus, she picks up her pace and runs all the way to Tray's house...

Knock-Knock-Knock... Tray open the door, it's me, Janey. *Knock-Knock-Knock*, what's going on, are you in there! *Then Janey smells a foul odor coming from the home—the smell is unfamiliar—it's an odor she has never smelt before, Janey gets frightened and calls her brother Derek for assistance.*

Ring-Ring-Ring...
Derek, it's me, I'm at a payphone near Tray's house—can you please come over; I think something is wrong. Tray never made it to the track and field event this weekend, and I smell a strange odor coming from inside her house—can you please meet me here?
Of course. Keep your cool lil sis. I'll be there in 20 minutes or less, just relax; I'm on my way. *Janey tries to wait patiently as her brother drives to meet her.*

Derek, thank God you made it, please help me. Tray never made it to the track meet this weekend, and I think something is wrong. *Derek notices the smell instantly, and the sent is familiar to him.* Tray-Tray are you in there, *Derek yells in a panic. The neighbors hear the fuss, and they call the cops, assuming Derek and Janey are trouble; thus, up to no good.*

That's it; I'm kicking the door down, back up Janey, get out of the way. *Two kicks later, and the door is off the hinges.* Wait at the door Janey, let me see what's going on inside the house, don't come in unless I say so.
Okay, Derek, be careful.

A few moments later. Damn, what the fuck, Derek utters loudly.
Derek, are you okay, what is it? I'm coming in... Oh, my God—Oh, my God. Tray-Tray; Oh, my God. No-no-no-no. *Janey touched the body, and the summer heat already started decomposing the flesh. Janey still isn't 100 percent from her recent illness; thus, she faints from*

despair. The police arrive within five minutes, and the ambulance is called, Janey is taken to the hospital, and Derek was taken in for questioning.

This is officially a crime scene, the officer stated, no one touches a thing. Seal the area; forensics are on their way.

Chapter 6: Aftermath

Get off me—get off me! Where is my brother? Derek, where are you? Janey yelled with fear and confusion when she regained consciousness.

Relax, Miss—take a deep breath and relax, you're in the ambulance; we're taking you to St. Sini hospital; you fainted 30 minutes ago and hit your head pretty hard when you went down. You'll be okay, but you most likely have a mild concussion, so please try to remain calm.

What…what happened to Tray? Is she… is she dead?

Yes, Miss, I'm afraid so—it appears she was deceased for at least three days. *Tears start falling down Janey's face; she's becoming hysterical and starts to blame herself.*

I knew I should have never let a minor stomach bug stop me from going to the Maryland track and field event; this is all my fault. If I met Tray at her house as planned, she would be alive today; I blame myself—I could have prevented this. I could have… wait, I know who killed her, that motherfucker John, I want to talk to the cops, now!

Don't worry about that, the paramedic declared. An officer is following behind the ambulance—a detective, as a matter of fact—and she has lots of questions for you. Your brother, Derek, is already at the police station, giving them information about the discovery.

What, why has my brother been detained, he didn't do anything wrong?

Your brother is not in any trouble; the officer wanted to get a statement from him; that's all—they will drive him to the hospital after they're done questioning him.

My brother has his own car; he can drive himself.

Okay, take it easy. Don't get yourself worked up again—we are a few minutes from the hospital, the detective will have questions and information for you when we arrive.

Janey complains of a headache—and she starts to feel faint; her blood pressure is elevating—its dangerously high, and her nose starts to bleed. She feels lightheaded, and her vitals are all over the place; thus, the paramedics give her a sedative to calm her down.

**** ****

At the Emergency room. What... what happened, where am I, what's going on?

Young lady, you're at St. Sini hospital, you hit your head when you collapsed. Once you regained consciousness, you became agitated and anxious—your vitals were all over the place; thus, the paramedic gave you Diazepam in the field. You may feel a little drowsy from the sedative, but don't worry; the side effects will dissipate very soon. We have you on IV fluids, which will flush the meds out of your system in no time. Your head looks fine; we gave you a cat scan while you were under; you're going to be okay.

Thank you, nurse, thank you very much.

You're welcome. By the way, there's a detective outside; she has a few questions for you, I'll let her in—if that's okay with you? Please use your call button if you need anything, I'll be right outside at the nurse's station.

Okay, nurse. Thank you, I will.

Hello, Janey, my name is Detective Price. I have a few questions for you about your friend Tray. When was the last time you spoke to her and/or saw her? *Janey starts speaking very fast; she gave Detective Price a mouth full—Janey went on and on.* Calm down; you're going to get yourself worked up again. Let's start from the top—when was the last time you spoke to Tray? Do you know if she was home alone when you talked to her on the phone? Was Tray likely to lie to you and her mom and have a boy over because her mother was out of town? *Janey gets upset with the line of questioning and asserts,* Hell no, Tray is not one of those types of girls, she like boys in all, but the track team is her life, nothing came before tract, nothing. Tray will never ditch a track meet just so that she could have the house to herself and be with a boy…

Okay, sounds good. I spoke with Tray's mom Ava, and she is headed back into town. Ava said everyone was away for the weekend, and her fiancé John was in New York for a bachelor party? Yes, detective, that is true, but John was at the house when I spoke with Tray on the phone—he never made it to NYC. He's your prime suspect, that bastard molested Tray a few months ago, and I believe he has something to do with her death—find that bastard and question him, start there.

Excuse me; John did what now, the detective uttered with shock?

Yes, that's right, John drugged Tray with Chloroform and sexually assaulted her, and she begged me not to say anything. My brother Derek had a not so pleasant conversation with John, and John said he would never do it again. Because of the assault, Tray and her little sister Beverly stayed at my house every night, for months. In fact, they recently moved back home.

This is pertinent information, the detective asserted—you rest now, I have some calls to make—and thank you for your help. *Detective Price left the room to follow up on the discoveries.*

Mumford "88"

Chapter 7: The Investigation

Ms. Ava, I have additional questions for you, *Detective Price had no problem getting straight to the point.* Are you aware that your fiancé John has been accused of sexually assaulting your daughter a few months ago?
What, excuse me, no way, that cannot be true. John will never do anything like that, who told you that awful lie?
According to Janey, John assaulted and drugged Tray with Chloroform a few months ago. Janey is in the hospital but gave me the okay to give you her room number or phone number so you can reach out to her. I need to know the whereabouts of John and the hotel he is staying at in New York City. I need that information now, please!
Detective Price is on the move; she's not wasting any time locating John and following up on the accusations.

Mumford "88"

Hello, forensics, this is Detective Price, check for traces of semen and chloroform, let me know when you have the results, please put a rush on everything, thank you… Hello, Stanyard Hotel, this is Detective Price, I need to know if you have a reservation for a Mr. John Peko, can you please confirm his booking?

Okay, mam, let me check the system... It appears we do not have a John Peko reserved here.
Okay please check for Mark Twain, maybe the reservation is under his name, he's the groom.
Okay, another moment, please... Yes, I have a Mark Twain reserved here.
Wonderful, I know it's late, but can you please connect me to his room?
Sure, right away, detective!

Ring-Ring-Ring…
Hello, *Mark answers the phone half-drunk from a night of partying.*
Hello, is this Mark Twain? Yes, it is, who's calling?
Hello, Mr. Twain, I'm Detective Price, I'm trying to get a hold of Mr. John Peko, would he happen to be there and/or did you see him tonight?
No, Detective, I'm sorry, John never showed.
Please hold. *Detective Price put Mark on hold and puts an APB (all point bulletin) on John and his vehicle.* Okay, Mark, I'm back, have you heard from John at all?
Yes, I spoke with John a few days ago when he was at his fiancé Ava's house—we spoke around 10:45-11 a.m., he said he was grabbing a few items, and he would be on the road by noon. But he never arrived, and he never called the hotel to leave a message. I figured his fiancé Ava made him go on the trip to the shore with the family.

Thank you so much, Mark, you have been very helpful—please take down my number and call me if John reaches out to you or if you remember anything else.
Okay, detective, I will. Can you please tell me what this is regarding?
I'm sorry, Mr. Twain, at this moment I cannot, but I'm sure you will hear about it within the coming hours, goodbye.

Mumford "88"

Ring-Ring-Ring...

Hello, Ava, this is detective Price, I want to inform you that John never made it to New York City. Have you heard from him at all this evening? I know it's the wee hours of the morning, but do you have any idea where he may have gone? Where he feels safe?

Yes, John is from San Diego, that is where his family and friends live. His mother's name is Pat, and she can be reached at this number.

Thank you, Ms. Ava. If you hear anything from John, call me any time of the day or night.

Okay, I will. Thank you, detective Price, I will do just that. *Ava tries her best to keep her composure so she can cooperate with the detective. Ava is distraught, and her heart is aching from the loss of her daughter. It's been over 24 hours since the discovery, and no one has heard from John, not even his mother.*

Chapter 8: The Arrest

Pull-over! Pull-over the vehicle right now! *Finally, a visual on John and the police proceed with caution.* Turn the ignition off, throw the keys out of the window, and slowly open the car door. *John complies.* Lift your hands out of the car, then slowly exit the vehicle... *The officers approach John, informs him that he's the primary suspect in the murder of Tray, then takes John into custody for questioning. John is devastated that the police were able to find him so swiftly. Now sober, John cannot believe the brutal crime he committed... Detective price is at the station waiting, along with Ava, Janey, and Derek.*

John's arrival at headquarters. Mr. Peko, my name is detective Price, and I'm the lead detective in the Tray X murder; thus, you're going to see a lot of me. I have many questions for you, but before we get started, would you like some water? You're going to be in this room for *quite some time!*

Yes, please. Water would be lovely; thank you very much for offering. *Detective prices nod her head carelessly—then leave the room to get John some water.*
So, John, can you tell me where you were on Thursday, July 28, 1988?
Yes, mam. I was headed out of town to a bachelor party. My friend Mark was getting married on Sunday, July 31st, but I never made it to the wedding. I ran into an old girlfriend from college, and we hooked up for the weekend; I was confused about the engagement to me fiancé Ava. Running into my college sweetheart left me with a bunch of repressed yet happy memories; thus, I decided to drive home to San Diego to clear my head.
Is that why you were in Indiana when the police officers located you yesterday evening?
Yes, detective. I figured I'd drive to California—which gave me time to clear my head, opposed to taking an airplane back home. *John's a fool—he thinks detective price believes his lie.*

John, I'm having trouble believing your statement, you wouldn't give false information to a law enforcement agent, would you? Do you know its a crime to withhold pertinent information?
Yes, mam, I do—and I would never lie to an officer or anyone else, that is, I'm an honest man...
Is that right? John listen up, I spoke with your friend Mark Twain, and he told me that he spoke with you around 10:45 a.m., on Thursday morning—phone records confirmed a call coming from Ava's home—to Marks hotel suite in New York City. Was that you?
No detective, I did not speak with John at all on Saturday, that wasn't me.
John, I believe you are lying to me, be honest, and maybe we can help you—maybe we can cut you a deal... Did you...... *at that moment, Officer Kelly entered the interrogation room to inform Detective Price that she has an urgent call.*

Hello, this is detective price, who am I speaking with?
Hello, detective, this is Dr. Smith from forensics. I wanted to inform you that we found trace elements of chloroform in the victim's system—we also found skin underneath her nails, as well as semen, and a blood type that wasn't her own. It appears our young victim put up quite a fight before she perished...
I love when an assailant leaves evidence behind, it makes my job so much easier. Thank you so much, Dr. Smith, for your prompted analysis, I will be in touch. *Detective price is furious—and*

she is pretty sure who committed the crime. The story Janey told her matches the forensic evidence Dr. Smith discovered.

John, I'm tired of playing around with you, I'm going to ask you again—did you kill Tray X, and leave her body at her mother's home to rot? Furthermore, did you rape Tray a few months ago, and drug her with chloroform?

Absolutely not! *John loses his cool for a second.* I would never do such a thing; I'm no rapist; these accusations are absurd. You're barking up the wrong tree; you have the wrong person…

No, I'm pretty sure we have the right guy. John, I'm placing you under arrest; we have DNA evidence from the crime scene, and I believe you're a match. Until forensic rules you out, I must detain you. I also believe you're a flight risk; thus, I will recommend that bail be denied. I'm sure you were headed out of town with hopes of ditching a murder rap. I do not believe your story about hooking up with your high school lover, but if you give me her name and number, I will do my due diligence and follow up on your claim, wrongful arrests are not my motto…

These charges are bullshit; my lawyer will have your badge, detective.

We will see about that Mr. Peko. The forensic evidence retrieved from Tray will either clear you or convict you. Time will tell… Until then, officer Kelly, book his ass!

With pleasure, detective!

Before John was taken into custody, detective Price allowed Ava to have a few words with her now former fiancé. Ava was pissed, but she still had doubts about the accusation detective price told her. However, once she spoke with Janey—as they waited for John to be delivered from Indiana, it became clear what John had done—and Ava couldn't believe how blind she was. Ave gave John a mouth full and followed her words with a solid and hard sucker punch—to John the sucker, bam!

A few days later. Hello, detective Price… this is Dr. Smith, again. I'm calling to notify you that the DNA you submitted for analysis—is a 99% match to the evidence we retrieved from young Tray's body. The forensics links John Peko to the crime.

Thank you, Dr. Smith. I trust the prosecution can use you as their forensic specialist at trial?

Yes, of course, detective; absolutely. *The one thing about forensics is that it never lies.*

Chapter 9: Come to Terms

As the community awaits trial, Janey has a hard time coping with the fact that Tray is no longer walking this earth—it's a hard pill to swallow because they were best friends since preschool. Janey blames herself for not reporting the crime to the police when Tray initially informed her of the incident; she also wishes red flags went off when Tray ended their last conversation with "I think John just walked in." Needless to say, Janey slipped into a mild depression. These are the five stages of grief: Denial, Isolation, Anger, Bargaining, Depression, and Acceptance. People in grieving do not necessarily follow a specific order or experience the same symptoms; individual results vary.

If I didn't go on that date with Bobby, I would have been around to stop the incident, or if I had ordered something else besides sushi, I wouldn't have been too sick to drive to Maryland with Tray. This is all my fault; I could have prevented this, Janey declares to her mother in agony. Don't beat yourself up, dear; you had no way of knowing John was going to hurt your friend; take it easy on yourself. I'm sure Tray wouldn't want you to drown in your sorrows. Tray would want you to find a way to continue living, and she would want you to be happy, despite it all.

Mumford "88"

Your right mom, but the reality is hard to face—it feels like a bad dream that I cannot wake up from. I can't shake the feeling that I could have prevented her death; that "only if" question keeps haunting me. You are experiencing the stages of grief, give it time—and you will learn how to deal with it, you *will* eventually find peace within.
Okay, mother, I will try, thank you for listening, as always, I appreciate you.
Of course, dear. You know I'm always here for you, no matter what. I love you, Janey.
I love you too, mom. *Janey and her mother embraced in a warm and loving hug.*

****

Later that evening. Derek, how are you holding up? I know Tray was like a sister to you. I overheard you and your boys talking in the basement yesterday evening—the conversation sounded heated. Are you having regrets about how you handled John many months ago?
Janey, I keep telling you not to worry about me, it's my job to worry about you and mom, I'll be fine lil sis. But yeah, I'm kicking myself in the ass for going soft and not killing that fool when I had the chance—your input affected my better judgment, but that won't happen again.

No, Derek, that's not true—I'm going to use the same phrase mom just used on me—It's not your fault—you had no idea it would come to this. Besides, if you would have killed John months ago—you would have had regrets about doing that too; you most likely would have doubted the murder by saying, "maybe there could have been another way, maybe I reacted too harshly, etc." Besides, Tray was thankful for your actions; she was grateful you did not kill John. Honestly, I don't think Tray would have been able to handle being the cause of someone's death, you know how Tray is, she's a lover of life—*was* a lover of life.

How did you get to be so smart sis, you have amazing strength, don't let this incident stop you from thriving—keep that happy spirit and joy for life. Do it for Tray, do it for others who may experience similar situations. I often imagine you being an advocate for others; it's in your soul.
Aww, you so sweet... Thank you, Derek, for always being supportive and having my back.
You're welcome, Janey, that's what big brothers are for. I will *always* have your back!
Communication is the key. All Janey needed was a healthy and loving conversation with her mother and brother—and her depression started to subside. Within 24 hours of talking with her

family, Janey was able to take a jog to Penn's Landing. The run felt good, and she felt Tray's spirit in the wind. In fact, Janey had an Idea; I will keep Tray's dream alive—I will join the track team in my senior year of high school and apply to colleges just as Tray did. *The idea of going to college was motivation and inspiration, and Janey was no longer drowning in her sorrows, she had something she needed and wanted to accomplish, something she desperately wanted to see manifest. The depression phase is over, Janey is on a mission—a mission to keep Tray's vision alive!*

****

A few weeks later. Tray this is for you, Janey uttered softly to herself—tomorrow is the hiking trip, and I will go on the trip knowing that you are near in spirit, I will *not* stop living, I will *not* let John's punk ass win. So, let's do this—let's go and enjoy the hiking trip before our senior year of high school begins—we *will* survive and become who we always thought we'd be. Can I get an Amen! *Janey isn't insane; she's aware she's talking to herself; she's merely thinking out loud and going with the intuition of the universe.*

The infamous hiking trip. Hey Janey, how are you holding up, I'm surprised you were able to make the trip, but we are happy that you are here? Everyone was heartbroken when we heard about what happened to Tray, are you okay, do you need anything?
I'm okay, Erica, and I don't need anything. *Erica is the elected head and speaker for the senior class of 1989.* I'm hanging in there; I decided to keep on living, never will I let the actions of another stop me from attending this event. Tray and I were looking forward to this trip all summer. Besides, I had a few weeks to dwell on the incident, and I decided to come as a tribute to Tray, this is what she would have wanted.
Wow, Janey, that's amazing—you are so strong, I commend your devotion to Tray. Oh, that reminds me, I have a surprise for you. Wait for a second; I want to gather everyone around so that they can hear this too.

Everyone listen up, Erica stated, Mumford High is dedicating the hiking trip to Tray X. In fact, the faculty decided to rename the annual senior trip *Tray X Hike Off to Senior Year*. This revision of name is to honor Tray, forever and for always. She was loved and respected by many of her peers; she was a great role model and a spectacular athlete, Tray this is for you, may you rest in peace, my dear.

Wow, I love it, Janey proclaimed. Thank you, Erica, thanks everyone, I'm sure Tray would've been honored, I'm speechless. *A tear of Joy was released from Janey's eye...* With that being said, I hope everyone has an amazing weekend, filled with joy, laughter, and many great memories—now, let the fun begin! *Everyone had a great time at the hiking trip; they celebrated and enjoyed the weekend—in memory of Tray. They kept her name in their prays before and after every meal, and they even put together a mindfulness meditation session in Tray's honor. It truly was a weekend to remember—completely dedicated to the late and great Tray X.*

Mumford "88"

Chapter 10: All in the Family

Hello, class of 1989! Welcome to your final year of high school! For those who do not know me, my name is Mrs. Jackson, and I will be your homeroom teacher the entire year. Welcome all, it is a pleasure to have each and every one of you in my class, let's make it a great year!

I'm so happy I have Mrs. Jackson for my homeroom teacher—she's caring, she's supportive of innovative ideas, and so helpful towards us students. Mrs. Jackson is a teacher who sincerely cares about her student's future. I have a feeling; in fact, I know this is going to be a great year, Erica uttered with enthusiasm.

Yes, Erica, you are correct, I get that same vibe from Mrs. Jackson. Despite everything that happened, I have a good feeling too. When I looked at my class schedule and saw her name as my homeroom teacher, a feeling of relief overcame me. Did you know that Mrs. Jackson was the only teacher who came to Tray's memorial, besides coach Trench or course? It's a joy to be in her classroom.

Mumford "88"

Yeah, it's a delight—and to be in the same homeroom with you, Janey, is "two strokes of luck for me. Last year, I didn't have any classes with you or Tray—and we had different lunch blocks; I was bored to death talking to some of these high school girls. It was almost impossible to engage in intellectual conversation. All they wanted to talk about was boys and clothes; like that's all there is to being a teenager. But this year, I can finally engage in decent conversations. Thank you, Erica, you're too kind. Oh, guess what—I'm signing up for the track team this year, I always took joy in running with Tray, but I never wanted to be on a formal team; to me, that took the joy out of the activity. But I will run this year, for Tray. I'm also going to fill out college applications with hopes of getting accepted into a few good universities based on my athletic abilities—who knows; I might get in. I figured it wouldn't hurt to try, and I can use the distraction.

That's great, go for it, Janey; you definitely have the grades and the athletic abilities to get into a decent university, Erica said supportively. I will have your back; I promise to be at every single practice, and track and field meet. I'll support you the way you supported Tray.

Wow, really. Thank you, Erica; I appreciate that—you're the best!

****🐒****

A few weeks later. Guess what, Derek, I made the track team; can you believe it? I got in!
Of course, I can believe it, that's what's up, Janey; I never doubted you would make the team, not even for a second. You and Tray ran like fanatics, non-stop training... *At that moment, Janey visualized the day she and Tray debated over which one of them was more fanatical...* You always had the talent, I'm proud of you sis, and I'm happy you decided to share your athletic abilities with the world.

Thanks, bro, I'm happy I decided to join the team; I'm super excited and looking forward to my first practice. I also like being around Coach Trench, he's so supportive, and he reminds me of Tray—and I can tell that I provide comfort to him as well, Tray was his fastest, hence, favorite runner you know.

A few moments later. Mom-mom, I made the track team, I was one of their top picks—I'm so thrilled mother, I didn't think I would make it, with this being my senior year of high school and

Mumford "88"

all. Usually, they don't allow new teammates in the senior year—unless there a transfer student who was previously on a track team... I hope nepotism didn't get me in.

Janey, you're a star, and coach Trench is aware of how hard you have been practicing with Tray—that is why you were accepted on the team. Besides, Mumford High would have been crazy not to pick you—you're dedicated and work hard at your goals, nepotism has nothing to do with your acceptance, remember that, sweetheart... How about we go out to celebrate your accomplishments? Let's go to Pandora's Café and get a hot meal; I don't have to work a 12-hour shift at the hospital tonight, what do you say?

I say, heck yeah; thanks, mom, I would love that!

Hey, I'm coming too, I'm hungry as a mug, Derek said...

Derek, you're all up in our business, Janey said playfully; I thought you were in the kitchen talking on the phone to your girlfriend.

Yeah, I was, but then I heard food, so here I am.

Okay, Kids, knock it off, we all can go. But Derek, we will ride in your SUV, my four-door Honda Accord is too small... Okay, mom, that's cool, but Honda's are not small.

Maybe not, but they're no SUV either...

True that, Derek agreed, true that!

You guys are crazy—I don't care who car I get in, Janey said, I'm hungry—and now my mouth is watering for Pandora's, let's go. Oh, wait, where is Kimmy, mother?

I took her on a play date with Beverly, she was asking for Bev—and Ava said she could use the distraction, and I needed a break...

Oh, wow, that's great. Thanks, mom, for allow Kimmy to go to Ms. Ava's house after all that occurred. I have to get over there myself; I still haven't seen the new house yet.

Of course, dear, the threat is in prison now—and yes, you have to see the new house; It's adorable, small but cute.

Enough with the charming house talk, Derek uttered humorously. I'm happy John Peko is lock away where he belongs, and hopefully, he isn't having a peaceful prison stay. The people in jail don't play when it comes to child molester and murders. He will get what he deserves, I'm sure of it, Derek proclaimed in a shrewd tone.

Mumford "88"

Derek, what do you have up your sleeves, don't get yourself into any trouble, boy. You are not too old to get a beaten form your momma! *Janey laughs subtly.*

I don't have anything up my sleeves, mother—I'm a good son. I'm just happy John is in jail where he belongs, that's all!

Janey laughs again.... She knows her brother has a dark side.

****

Chapter 11: The Restaurant

I love coming to this restaurant, mother, thanks for bringing us. It's not that crowded tonight either, and the aroma smells divine, I cannot wait to eat. There's nothing like the smell of fresh-baked bread when entering an eatery, Janey asserted.

Your right about that, Derek agreed. But as you'll wait for a table, I'm going to hit the tavern section and get me a bourbon. I'm 21, so I can legally drink.

Derek, only have one cocktail. I don't want to have to drive your oversized SUV home after dinner; you're not a heavy drinker. Remember your birthday party, two shots of bourbon, and you were tipsy and dancing with *all* the ladies.

Okay, mom, thanks for reminding me, as if I could forget. That was a hell-of-a party, by the way; it was so much fun, my best birthday by far. *They reminisced on Derek's birthday party and how he danced with the ladies and started laughing, it was hilarious.*

Mumford "88"

A few minutes later. Your table is ready... please follow me, the attendant asserted. Please have a seat and review the menu; I will be back shortly with water and fresh bread...

Thank you, everyone asserted simultaneously.
The dinner menu has so many delicious options, its hard to choose, but I know what I want. I'll have the sautéed broccoli and salmon entree, Janey asserted.
Oh, that sounds delicious; I'll have the same...
Mom, you're always copying off me, are you sure you want broccoli and salmon?
Yeah, Janey. I want the broccoli and salmon entree—I want to try something different, I'm tired of chicken or veal—and who cares what I order, I'm paying for the meal.
Derek chuckles... mom roasted you; she put you in your place real nice! And mom, I'm going to order the steak dinner, if that is okay? *Derek was being playful and funny.*
Of course, it's okay, dear, order whatever you want. Gorge oneself, it's a special evening!

Derek, your appetite is hearty; your always ordering beef products; that's why your growing like a weed. I cannot believe how tall you are; you're what, 6'2'' now? I remember when you graduated from High school, you were only 5'9."
Well, Janey, what can I say—I'm a growing man, and protein is needed to build all these muscles; also, I like to eat so mind your business, big-head!
Kids settle down. So, Janey, tell me about college—what schools are you applying for?
I'm applying for the same universities Tray was accepted into. I'm only going to college to keep Tray's dream alive. My goal is to open my own clothing store. "Sexy w/ Class Fashion Boutique." But first I want to try out this college thing, for the sake of Tray, that is.
That's right, sis, your own clothing boutique, self-employment is the way to go.

I'm so proud of you, honey. You and your brother have made me a proud parent... So, Derek, how are things going with your business, is it still thriving at an accelerated pace?
Yes, it is mother. Everything is great with *Derek's, Media, and Photography Productions!* I have clients throughout the Tri-States, and my business is spreading to Baltimore, Maryland, and DC. I hired three new guys; the business is doing well. And, I don't have a huge student loan debt over my head. That's right, no student loan payments for me...
What.... So, what are you trying to say, Derek? Is that a roast at me, Janey said with a smile...?

Mumford "88"

No, lil sis, darn. Besides, I know you're applying for scholarships, just like Tray, no student loan debt for you either. You're a smart girl; I know you got this!
A few moments later. Hey, Janey, isn't that Bobby over there; it looks like he's on a date.
Where? Oh yes, that's him, I haven't called him since the incident happened. And we only went on one date, so he has the right to date other people. I'm going to say hello; I'll be right back.

Hello, Bobby, how are you?
Bobby turned around and quickly stood up and said, Janey, how are you! I'm so sorry to hear about Tray; she was an amazing person. I called you several times, but your mother said you weren't available, I even came to the funeral.
Sorry about that, Bobby, I was out of it for a few days, but I'm better now...
That's good to hear Janey; I was worried about you. Oh, where are my manners, Tabitha this is Janey; Janey, this is Tabitha—we're having dinner...
Yes, I can see that. Hello Tabitha, nice to meet you.
Hello Janey, it's nice to meet you also. I've heard a few good things about you from Bobby...
Is that right, Janey said as she looked at Bobby intriguingly.
Excuse me, Tabitha, may I have a word alone with Janey?
Sure, go right ahead... *Bobby gently pulled Janey to the side and offers her words of comfort. He's also apologizing for being out on a date.*
Bobby, it's okay, we only been out on one date, and I don't know if you heard, but that date put me in the hospital...
What. No, I haven't heard, are you okay?
I am now, but that sushi restaurant you took me to, served some questionable seafood—do not take me there ever again.
Oh, wow, so does that mean your willing to go out with me again? *All Bobby heard was, "do not take me there ever again," and rounded that up to he will get a second date with Janey.*
It depends, but maybe... I'm definitely not upset with you for being out on a date—I've seen Tabitha around town; she appears to be a lovely girl. Let's see what the future holds regarding our second date...
Okay, Janey, that sounds good to me, have a good evening with your family—please tell your mother and brother hello for me...

Mumford "88"

I sure will. Maybe I'll see you around; have a good evening.
Thanks, you too!

Mom, Derek—Bobby asked me to tell you both hello. *At that moment the waiter arrives with their meals.*
Great, perfect timing—I'm starving, Derek said.
Me too, Janey agreed; let's eat—but first, I want to say a prayer for Tray. *"God, I want to thank you for giving everyone the strength to come to terms with the tragedy that recently occurred. It was a rough road, and we still have hard times ahead of us—with the trial in all, but I thank you for getting us this far. May I make Tray proud by living my life in compliance with her very own. And may I not lose sight of my own dreams along the way, Amen."*
Amen. That was a beautiful prayer, Janey...
Thanks, mom!
Now let's eat, Derek uttered. *Janey and her family had a peaceful dinner at Pandoras Café.*

Later that evening. Thanks, again for the meal mother, I had a great time...
Your welcome, dear. And thank you, Derek, for leaving a sizable tip for the waiter...
It's called teamwork mother. I know you could have paid for everything, but I wanted to contribute to celebrating Janey's big night, our future track star, my big head little sister is going to do great things!
Yeah, I am. Lol. Okay, mom and Derek, thanks again for a great evening, but I'm going to rest for a little then get changed and go down to the basement to work off that delicious meal. You know I have to burn off those calories. Now that I'm on the track team, I don't want to get out of shape.
Okay. Sounds good to me, dear.

Even later that evening. Knock-knock-knock...
Who is it?
It's Bobby, Ms. Brooks, is Janey home?
Sure, come in while I get her, she's in the basement working out; you can wait in the kitchen...

Mumford "88"

Janey, dear, you have company!

I do, who is it, mom?

It's Bobby...

Bobby, what is he doing here, shouldn't he still be on his date with Tabitha?

I guess he cut it short—he's sitting in the kitchen waiting for you...

Okay, thanks, mom.

Hey, Bobby, what's up... what are you doing here?

Wow, Janey, you look great, amazing, I mean.... I'm sorry, but wow!

Boy, please, I'm all sweaty and stinky...

Sweat and funk look good on you, Janey...

Lol, you got game, what's up, Bobby—I have to finish training...

I just wanted to stop by and make sure you are doing okay, but it appears you are doing great. I also wanted to apologize for not making a harder effort to see you after our initial date and the Tray accident.

That's fine, I wasn't reachable, even if you tried, there was no way you were going to reach me.

Oh, I did try, I left three messages, but I gave up after that. But if I had known you were in the hospital because of the restaurant I took you to, I would have come to visit you and brought you flowers. I'm a gentleman, you know.

Yes, I know, which is why I went on that date with you. I don't date anybody...

Oh, I know, in fact, everyone in school knows that—and I respect the hell out of you for that...

Thanks, Bobby, but I must get back to my workout, I don't want my heart rate to slow down too much. I'll call you tomorrow...

I hope so, Janey; I hope so...

Goodnight, Bobby...

Oh, I almost forgot, I have something for you, Janey...

What is it? *At that moment, Bobby pulled a single red rose from behind his back...*

Aww, thank you so much—Tray was correct; you really are an amazing guy, I'm flattered...

Anything for you, Janey... *Janey smiles from ear-to-ear as they call it a night.*

****   ****

Chapter 12: The Trial Begins

All Rise, the court of honorable Judge Kingston, is now in session... You may be seated. Your honor, today's case is Commonwealth vs. John Peko.... *There is tension in the courtroom; everyone gathered inside courtroom 'F' to witness the trial of John Peko—positive he will be punished for his crimes...*

Presenting the case before you today, the defendant John Peko has been charged with the rape and murder of Tray X. The prosecution will prove that Mr. Peko brutally murdered and sexually assaulted Tray on Thursday, July 28, 1988.

The prosecution calls Dr. Emily Smith...

Hello, Dr. Smith, do you recall the forensic evidence detective Price submitted to your lab for analysis on Sunday, July 31^{st,} 1988?

Yes, I do. The victim had another person's skin underneath her nails; there were also foreign blood and traces of semen on the clothing she was wearing the day of the crime. We ran data analysis with the DNA provided to use—and it was a match to Mr. John Peko.

Thank you, Dr. Smith, for your testimony; you may leave the witness stand.

The prosecution now calls Serena Jones to the stand.

Hello Ms. Jones, what is your relationship with John Peko?

John was my boyfriend of four years before he left for the East Coast.

And what caused the separation, Ms. Jones?

It is believed that John made sexual advances towards my eleven-year-old daughter. When the authorities arrested John, he denied it. Regrettably, there was not any solid evidence, and the case was dismissed. Not long after the incident, John moved to the East Coast, and we never saw or heard from him again...

Ms. Jones, it is believed that Mr. Peko came to Philadelphia on a work-related assignment, is that true?

No, ma'am. John was fired from his job because of the accusations—he came to Pennsylvania "most likely" because he was hiding from the town gossip, which was a result of the allegations, I guess he wanted a fresh start...

"Objection," *the defense attorney shouted.* Ms. Jones doesn't know why my client came to the East Coast; she's speculating.

She said, "most likely," the reason why Mr. Peko came to the East Coast," *the prosecution uttered."*

"Overruled," *the judge asserted.*

Thank you, your honor... Thank you, Ms. Jones, that will be all. I have no further question for the witness at this time—you may leave the witness stand; *Ms. Jones nodded her head and left the stand—not once did she glance at John Peko.*

The trial went on for almost two weeks: The prosecution calls John Peko to the stand... Mr. Peko, where were you on Thursday, July 28th, 1988?

I was in Philadelphia when I ran into a dear old friend from high school, we spent the day together catching up and talking about "the good old days," and we ended up getting a hotel room for the night... Spending time with my high school sweetheart left me feeling uncertain about my life and my decision to marry Ava.

Mumford "88"

Mr. Peko, I tried calling your old girlfriend from high school, but the number your attorney provided us isn't working—the name and number seem to be fictional. You running into your high school sweetheart appears to be a lie, do you make a habit of lying Mr. Peko?
Objection! The prosecution is badgering the defendant, the defense attorney stated.
Overruled, please answer the question, the judge asserted.
No, I do not make a habit of lying, the number I gave the detective months ago—and the number my attorney provided to the prosecution *is* the number my friend from high school gave me, I'm sorry you're having trouble reaching her.
Your sorry I'm having trouble… the prosecution uttered, it appears no one can find this mystery woman, including your attorney. This "high school sweetheart" could make all your troubles go away—and the fact that she isn't reachable leaves me no choice than to believe you are lying!

So, Mr. Peko, let's move on to another question, *John was relieved because he was lying…* were you at your ex-fiancé's house the morning of July 28^{th,} 1988—and did you call Mark Twain the morning of Tray's death—I'm sorry, murder?
No, I did not make any calls that morning. My ex-fiancé Ava and I left the house early Thursday morning—at the same time, and I never returned. As I stated to you during the initial interview detective, I was confused after running into my high school sweetheart—and I was having doubts about "tying the knot." Mark was the last person I wanted to speak to, he was getting married that weekend, and I didn't want to talk to him about my doubts.

So, Mr. Peko, are you denying that it was you who made the call to Mark's hotel suite?
Yes, I refute that—the call didn't come from me…
So why do you suppose Mark claimed he spoke with you that morning?
I don't know; Mark was drunk all week; he was gaming up for a big bachelor party weekend, maybe he got me confused with someone else.
"Objection your honor," If John wasn't in New York City—and if he didn't speak to Mark, his statement insinuating that Mark was drunk *is* an assumption…
"Sustained," that is speculation—jury, please disregard that last statement, the judge asserted.

The trial went on and on; sadly, John was not going to admit that he had anything to do with Tray's death; he was in denial… The prosecution team was unrelenting, and they finally were able to track down John's high school sweetheart—and she confirmed she had, in fact, ran into John early Thursday morning. But it was brief, and she did not give him her phone number. She proclaimed that she told John she was happily married and was in town on business, and that was the last time she saw and heard from him... When everything was said and done, it took the jury less than one hour to find John Peko guilty of second-degree murder and rape. The family and community were pleased with the results. Two weeks after the trial concluded, John was sentenced to a State Penitentiary—where he will serve 25 years to life in prison.

****

Listen up, Derek uttered—John will serve his time at Hard-Knock-Life Penitentiary; I know a few tough guys in that jail. Many have three strikes under their belt; thus, they are serving life in prison—without the possibility of parole, and they will be happy to do me a favor or two. Long as I provide funds to their family, it's a done deal. *Derek is having a detailed and private conversation with his best boy Barry—they've been friends since second grade, and he is in on the plot.*

I'm ready to handle business, Barry declared. Just say the word, and I got you!
Derek makes a few calls and sends a large sum of funds to a certain inmate's family. The amount of funds determines the severity of the villainy. Anything under $10K means a severe beat-down for an extended amount of time—over a specific amount of years. Anything over $20K means murder—bye-bye-babe—and Derek and Barry sent way over $20K. John is marked.

It's a hard-knock life at the State Penitentiary. Are you John Peko, an inmate asked curiously? Yeah, that's me. Bam-Bam-Bam... *John is knocked-out-cold on the floor—two of his teeth laid beside him... A week later, in the shower, John was sexually assaulted, a crime he is very familiar with. John couldn't walk for over two weeks, and when he did, he had a limp and needed a cane... His meals were taken from him repeatedly; his stomach ached from starvation... Then finally, one day after a two month stretch in prison, John was strangled to death, but not before one final sexual assault, but no semen was left for forensics; this was a clean homicide. John is no more, and Ms. Ava and the rest of her family can live in peace, knowing that John is no longer on this earth—he will not be able to harm another child, ever again. Street justice has been served.*

****

Mumford "88"

Derek, did you hear about John? I heard he was killed in prison yesterday evening—his demise was similar to how Tray was murdered—I cannot believe it, John is dead. Oh well—karma.
Yeah, Janey, Karma. A person's actions often determine their destiny. John was a bad guy and made bad decisions—it was a matter of time before someone took him out. I didn't see a good outcome for him. Lifestyle often predicts outcomes. I guess someone from prison read the story in the newspapers and determined his fate would mirror the life he took—I don't feel sympathy for the basted; it was his time to leave this world, I guess.
Derek, did you have anything to do with his death, Janey asked curiously.
No, I did not, and if I did, a gentleman never tells, so don't ask again! *That was the only time Janey asked Derek if he was responsible for John's murder. Honestly, she didn't care, and she felt relief knowing that John won't be able to experience good days, speak to his family, or have the privilege of being alive. Eye for an eye, tooth for a tooth, life for a life—the circle of life.*

Chapter 13: Hello College

Hello, autumn 1989 and hello Pennsylvania University—Tray I cannot believe it, we did it, your dreams have come true. I'm in college with a full scholarship—long as I keep a high academic GPA, I'll have a free ride. *Janey was aware she was talking to herself—and merged her life and Tray's into one—but that was the point. Janey wanted Tray's memory to live vicariously through her; this kept Tray's vision alive, which helped her cope. Remember, Janey never wanted to attend college, that was Tray's dream—and Janey took pleasure in making Tray's dream a reality... Maybe in keeping Tray's dream alive, Janey will become all she ever wanted to be, plus so much more, or maybe she'll be full of regrets? Let's read on.*

It's the first weeks into the semester, and track and field events are already underway. Janey, I'm impressed with your speed, Coach Barnes asserted. I remember when Coach Trench invited me to attend one of Mumford High's legendary track and field events—I was blown away with your talent. And today, you claimed 2nd place in the 200-meter sprint—well done. I know your family is very proud of you? And I see a first-place ribbon in your near future.

Thank you, Coach, for all of the training, dietary tips, and words of wisdom. And yes, my family is super excited for me. I just want to make sure I do not disappoint them or you—and of course myself.

You couldn't disappoint me, Janey, even if you tried. Your efforts are what matters. After all, we cannot win them all. But the wins should outweigh the losses by far.

Thanks, Coach. And I'm determined to bring home a first-place ribbon at the next track meet; it's a personal goal for me!

I'm sure you will do it, Janey. Have a good day with your family and friends.

****

A few moments later. Hey Babe, you looked great out there on the field today, you had me going crazy in the bleachers. Did you hear us, did you hear it, the crowd went wild, you were so fast, Janey. You belong here; you're a star!

Thanks, Bobby. I'm happy you were able to make it to the University—and looking handsome as ever. I miss your face, your touch, and your delicious scent.

I miss you too, Janey, and are you kidding me—I wouldn't have missed your first track meet for anything in the world... *Yes, Bobby and Janey became a couple after they saw each other at Pandora's Café almost a year ago.*

Your mom, Derek, and Kimmy are on the other side of the bleachers getting refreshments, come on I'll take you to them; they went to get snacks, mainly water from all the shouting we did, our throats are parched—we need to hydrate.

Boy, please, my throat is super dry from all that running I did. Remember me; I was the one down there running on the field, burning in the hot ass sun?

You're hilarious, Janey. Yes, I remember. Don't worry; we're getting you some water also. Now kiss your man before your mom and brother return.

A few minutes later. Hey mom! I'm so happy to see you. Thanks for driving out here today, I know you have long workdays, but I'm so happy to see you, I miss you so much! And Derek and Kimmy, I'm so glad to see you guys too; it seems like I haven't seen everyone in forever.

Speaking of everyone, Janey's moms uttered... *everyone* did make it their priority to support you at your first college track and field event—and I mean *everyone*! *When Janey turned around, there was Ava and Beverly—smiling from ear-to-ear.*

Oh, my God. Oh, my God, thank you so much, Ms. Ava; I'm super thrilled to see you; thank you for coming, Oh, my God. I did not expect to see you here today; I'm so surprised...
Yes, and you look it—and you're welcome, Janey. You have made me very proud—my daughter would be so happy for you, *as tears rolled down Ava's face,* very proud. Thank you for keeping her dream alive—and with such passion and grace.
It's my pleasure, Ms. Ava. I feel Tray's presence when I'm out there on the field; her energy is all over me, pushing me to go further.
Derek clears his throat. Cocktails and lunch are on me, *Derek wanted to interrupt the sentimental moment before tears started falling down everyone faces...*
Yeah, I'm hungry Kimmy and Bev said—we would like hot dogs and chili fries from the Burger Palace, it's only three blocks away, they have really good milkshakes, can we go, please!
Sure, let's go, Ava said, but my treat—sorry, Derek, you can treat next time...
Next time, Janey uttered. So, this will become normality for you, Ms. Ava? Your coming to more of my track meets?
Absolutely. Yes, I will—if you'll have me, of course.
That would be wonderful; Tray would like that a lot, thank you so much! *There was a moment of silence, as realism sets in.*
Ms. Ava, despite it all, Tray loved you with all her heart and soul—that was the main reason she kept silent, she didn't want to hurt you, she wanted you to be happy—even if it caused her misery and pain...
Thank you for that Janey, I needed to hear those words; but as a mother, my children's happiness comes first. I wish Tray would have told me.
I know Ms. Ava, me too. And you're welcome. I should have told you sooner just how much Tray loved you, but I was hurting and didn't think to say it.
Bobby clears his throat.... Okay, Janey, I'll let you enjoy your time with your family, I'll chill in your dorm room until you're done.
Oh, no, Bobby, you're not getting off that easily, you are coming to eat with us, Derek stated...

Mumford "88"

If it's okay with everyone, it would be my pleasure to tag along. *It's fine with me; everyone uttered simultaneously.*

****🚩****

Later that afternoon. That was a great meal, just what I needed after two weeks of intense training and eating nothing but healthy foods, yummy. Thanks for treating everyone to a hearty meal Ms. Ava—and thank you all for supporting me today, I am grateful. I know you all must head back home, but I'm looking forward to seeing everyone on Halloween weekend. I cannot wait to attend the big haunted house extravaganza at the Mosholu; their costume contest is the best in the city!

I'm looking forward to it also; it's going to be fun, Janey's moms declared. Okay, dear, you have a good evening with your friends, give me a hug and kiss, sugarplum. We must go before the traffic gets bad—the interstate turns into a parking lot during the evening hours.
Mother, you want a kiss? You're embarrassing me in front of Bobby, *Janey disregarded everything about the traffic jam, all she heard was a hug and kiss.*
Oh, Bobby can have a hug too, Janey!
Mom guys don't hug, Derek said playfully...
Yeah, so your sister cannot have a hug before you leave campus, Janey teased.
Alright, get over here, big-head—show your brother some love. *Everyone laughs and giggles as they give each other hugs and kisses before they head to their cars and drive home.*

Mumford "88"

Chapter 14: The Night

So, Bobby, what time are you leaving later this evening? There's an off-campus party that starts around 8 p.m. Maybe you can hang around campus for a little while and tour the sights further, then check out the party before you head home! What do you think, are you down for that?
Yeah. Sure, that sounds like a plan to me... I get to spend more time with you, let's do it!
Okay, let's go to my dorm room and idle away time. I want to shower and relax for a while—then I'll get dressed for the evening. My roommate Sarah is there, so be nice, Bobby. No crazy jokes, or strange stories, she's sensitive.
What. Aren't I always nice? And telling jokes is what I do. I get it from my mother; she's half Italian, you know? And you know what they say about Italians and their jokes?
Yes, jokes *and* telling stories are their specialties. You know I adore you and your mom's tales—but Sarah can be sensitive and introverted at times, so please, easy on the conversation. If she engages in an elongated discussion, then your in; tell jokes till the morning comes...
I got you, Babe. I understand—I'll behave. *Bobby smiled, then there was a moment of silence as Bobby and Janey looked into each other's eyes.*

Mumford "88"

My goodness, Bobby, your hazel eyes got me mesmerized… *Janey was trying to shake off the sexual tension she was experiencing…* But on the real, I just wanted to say—you're the sweetest guy I know. I appreciate you and your patience with me; in all honesty, you're a good man...
Aww, and you're a good woman, I knew it from the moment I laid my hazel-brown eyes on you, *They both giggled.* Now let's head to your dorm, you have the three S's.
What's that, Bobby?
You need a shower, babe—you're "sweaty," "stinky," but "sexy"— and I must admit, I love them all! You can sweat on me any day of the week, babe.
You see Bobby; there it is—you know exactly how to tell me I smell funky, but then you throw in a compliment and make it sound cute and sweet, you're the best... *Once they arrived at Janey's dorm room, Janey showered, and they watched a movie with Sarah to consume time. Around 7 p.m., they decided to get ready for the evening.*

****🚿****

Hey, Bobby, you like my mini-skirt and my red halter-top, what do you think?
Wow, you look hot, you are as sexy as they come—and your legs in that outfit, stunning. You are *really* lean and fit, Janey, my god, you're super-hot!
Lol, you're so charming, Bobby, thanks. Oh, where did Sarah go? Her purse and shoes are gone. Her boyfriend came for her… they went to get something to eat before the campus party. But now that we have the room to ourselves, can I get a kiss? I mean a real kiss, it's about time you learn how to French kiss, Janey...
Umm, I think that will be okay. Show me, wait, tell me first. I need to hear how it's supposed to be done; I'm nervous, but ready to learn, Janey utters.

Okay, first and foremost, the moment must be there. Then you close your eyes and slightly open your mouth—gently kissing my lips—slowly moving your head left and right—play around for a little before you slip me the tongue if you decide to slip me the tongue… Keeping your lips soft and subtle. Oh, and easy on the saliva. Our tongues will intermingle as the kiss prolongs, and make noise if you desire, don't hold back…
Okay, that sounds simple enough, I think I can do that.

Mumford "88"

****

Bobby, how do I look? *Janey did a little swirl to show off her outfit, yet again.*
As you know, you are stunning babe, I mean wow, oh my God, I'm so in love with your sexy ass! *And this is the moment; they both lean forward—pause as they gaze into each other's eyes—and Janey's experiences her first French kiss—her knees get weak, and she stumbles into Bobby's arms—captivated by her first sexual kiss, she feels her love deepen for him... They both laugh for a few seconds before distancing their bodies. Though Bobby envisioned making love to Janey for the first time, then and there—but like the gentlemen he is, he held his composure.*

Mm-mm, that was so good, you're a great kisser, Bobby. We will have to do that again...
You won't get an argument from me on that—and you did well yourself, Janey. Your lips are soft and erotic; I may be coming in for kisses throughout the night, and not our normal peck...
Okay, we will see about that, Janey said nervously. So, as I was saying earlier, the party is at an off-campus location. Some college kids, mainly juniors and seniors, rent a house off-campus for the semester; it's more freedom I hear...
So, Janey, tell me—how does a freshmen college student get an invite to a seasoned campus party, your still novice?
Bobby, if you must know—it's my looks, I'm hot; isn't that what you said?
What...., Janey; you're crazy!
Sike, naw. It's because I'm an athlete. It doesn't matter what year you are—when a student plays sports for the university, their considered "the in-crowd." I'm a track star, did you not hear, 2nd place in the 200-meter sprint. But you know I'm training to be number one, right?
That's my girl; I love your drive... get them, Babe, you got this!

****

Later that evening. Wow, Janey, this party is off the hook— Pennsylvania University sure does know how to throw a party. And the music is different, I'm not used to it, yet it's really good!
Yeah, it is. I like college parties because the music genre is diverse; they play a little bit of

everything; that way, everyone can enjoy the event. Hey, since you like the music… do you want to dance, Bobby? Show me what you got!

Sure, you don't have to ask me twice, I came out to have a great time, so let's do this!

Wow, I didn't know you were such an amazing dancer, Bobby—you got some skills…

You're not so bad yourself, now give me a quick peck on the lips, Janey. Your lip gloss has your lips looking sexy and juicy as ever, or maybe I'm just reminiscing on that kiss from earlier today, either or, I want those juicy lips on mine. *Janey abides and kisses her man soft, short, and subtly.*

Later that evening. Hey, Bobby, they're playing a trivia game in the other room; whoever answers wrong must take a shot—you want in, you want to give it a go?

Sure Janey, let's see how smart college students really are; I'm in.

Okay, Bobby, but don't forget if you get a question wrong, you must take a shot of vodka, rum, or tequila. So, take your time and answer the questions wisely.

Okay, Janey. My IQ is high, and I can handle my liquor; I got this...

I know you're smart, Mr. Police academy, and I'm sure you can handle your liquor. I'm projecting my reality on you because alcohol goes straight to my head. So, I cannot lose more than twice, three times max. I get tipsy, way too fast—I want to enjoy and remember the night, so I'm going easy on the liquor... You see that girl over there in the corner; she's as drunk as a skunk, and I don't want that to be me tonight...

Sounds fair and smart to me, babe. Easy on the alcohol so that we can enjoy the night and remember it the next day.

It was a night to remember, Janey and Bobby had an amazing evening, filled with dancing, games, and laughter. And best of all, Janey did not get too wasted.

Time flies when you're having fun. Bobby, it's 1:30 a.m., the night went by fast. I know you can handle your liquor, but you had one too many drinks to drive home this late, and under the influence. There's no way I'm letting you drive home tonight.

Yeah, I know, I have my credit card with me; I'll check into the hotel two blocks away from campus. I'll walk you to your dorm room, and then I'll check into the hotel. Maybe we can have breakfast tomorrow morning before I head home.

Well, can I stay in the hotel with you?

Mumford "88"

Are you sure that's what you want to do, Janey? I mean, nothing's going to happen or anything, I know how you are with your reputation in all.
You're my long-term boyfriend, and I'm in college. I think I'm allowed to stay over without my reputation getting bruised.
Okay, to the hotel, it is.

****

Wow, this is a lovely room, much bigger than my dorm room. I feel comfortable already.
Yeah, it pretty cool, I love the color scheme, and that bed is extra-large, I'm going to sleep good tonight, I hope you don't mind snoring, Janey… *they both laughed; Bobby was kidding.*
So, Bobby, we talked about me all day, tell me how are things going in the police academy, hows your grades holding up?
Everything is good, and my GPA is excellent. I'm learning a lot of legal terms and descriptive codes—also, they make us train several times a week. Babe, I don't know how you do it, cardio training is hard, it's really intense. I be tired as fuck afterward!
Yeah, it is hard, but cardio is essential for the academy; you will have to chase bad guys now and then. I'm excited for you, Bobby; It sounds like you're enjoying the process of becoming a police officer, minus the cardio?
Yeah, it's a good pick for me, the Community College is perfect—and it's not expensive, so I'm paying for my education out of pocket, with the help of my parents, of course.
I heard that—no student loan debt sounds good to me. I'm happy your happy, Bobby…
And I'm happy your happy too, Janey. *Here's that moment again. They both lean forward and engage in a subtle, long, and meaningful kiss. Sacred Energy Exchange (s.e.x) is vibrating all over the room.* "It's about to go down," *Janey mumbles to herself.*
I hope she doesn't regret this in the morning; maybe I should stop this, Bobby thinks.

Hey Janey, hold off a second, this is getting heated. Are you sure you want to go through with this? Are you sure you want to go to "home-base?"
Maybe, I think so…

Mumford "88"

I want you to *know* so. I want you to *be* sure. So, let's stop this and watch a little TV before we doze off. I will never rush you to do anything you're not ready for. Just because we have this hotel room, doesn't mean we have to have sex tonight. I love you regardless, and you know that. Yes, I do. You're amazing. Thank you, Bobby. Okay, sounds like a plan—I'm going to take a quick shower, all that dancing made me sweaty and funky, again. *They both chuckled.*
Okay, and I'll get in after you, take your time, babe.
Janey is in the shower, thinking about what just happened—and is completely at Aww with Bobby's level of patience with her. Bobby is lying on the bed—just watching sports—nothing particular is going through his mind...

All done, Bobby, you can head into the shower now...
Okay, great, don't change the channel, I'll listen from the bathroom. I want to know who wins the game; it looks like my team might pull it off...
Okay, I won't switch the channel, I'm too tired to watch TV anyway. *Janey laid her head down on the pillow and was fast to sleep.*

Wow, she fell to sleep fast, Bobby uttered softly to himself when he exited the shower, guess she was tired—or maybe it was the alcohol or a mixture of the two, oh well. *Bobby watched the rest of the game before he drifts off to dreamland also.*

Good morning, Bobby. I slept great last night; this bed is so comfortable...
Yeah, it is very comfy—I slept like a baby. And just so you know, you were snoring by the time I was done with my shower last night.
What? I do not snore.
Babe, yes, you do! *Janey hits him with a pillow—then she uses the restroom to wash her face and brush her teeth. In the bathroom, Janey reminisces about last night.*

A few moments later. So, Bobby, about last night....
What's that, babe. What's on your mind?
I'm positive....

Mumford "88"

Huh, what, positive about?
Yes.... *At that moment, Janey slipped off her T-shirt and climbed on top of Bobby as he laid on the bed—she had no idea what she was doing, but she went with the flow—Sacred Energy Exchange (s.e.x) lingered in the room. Bobby says, "what are you doing—are you sure?" And Janey doesn't say a word; she starts to kiss Bobby soft and subtle, the way he taught her yesterday evening. Bobby's manhood rises, and he starts whispering in her ear sweet nothings, and Janey enjoys the way his soft voice and kisses feel against her ear—thus, a soft and sexy moan escape her lips. Bobby's erection intensifies—and he flips Janey on the bed and starts to kiss her nipples as he fondles her breast, then he goes down to her tummy, inner thighs, then he softly licks her vagina. Janey lets out a not so subtly sigh and feels her body start to shake. This is her very first orgasm, she feels the blood rushing through her entire body—her heart is beating faster and faster—her body feels electrifying, sensational, she's in heaven—and then she releases a loud moan as her female excretions drip onto Bobby's lips and tongue. Oh my God, what the fuck was that—oh my God, that was amazing—Jesus fucking Christ....*

Are you okay, Bobby whispered?
Yes. I've never been better, that was amazing, Janey softly uttered after a couple of seconds of silence—she needed to catch her composure.
That was also fast, babe; it took less than five minutes total for you to climax—I'm impressed with my skills...
Boy, be quiet, that was my first time—and I had built up sexual tension, so I climaxed fast. Plus, it felt so fucking good. Mmmm, amazing...

It makes me feel good knowing that I satisfy your desires. And trust me when I say, your pussy tastes good, and I enjoyed the fuck out of licking your clitoris; yummy, so delicious. But Janey, it's still your first time, we haven't had sexual intercourse yet, we only made it to "third base."
Oh, I know, Bobby—we're not done yet, I'm just getting started, it's your turn. I want to taste your dick and feel how hard you get inside my mouth; my jaws are watering, I'm ready...
No, don't do that, Janey, I don't want you moving too fast. You don't have to perform oral sex on me because I licked your warm, tight, and delicious vagina; that was my pleasure. Let's take it slow and easy; we have all the time in the world.

Mumford "88"

I love you, Bobby, your amazing. Now I'm yearning to feel your dick inside me.
I'm longing for you too, Janey, more than you'll ever know. And I love you too. But we can save some things for later down the line; I'm not going anywhere, babe. I'm here to stay.

Bobby leans forward to kiss Janey, then he whispers in her ear—I want you to be okay. I love your smile, your body, your laugh, your touch, and now the taste of your pussy... Janey moans again and says, "Oh, my god, I'm so wet, put it in." Bobby asks one more time, "are you sure," and Janey says, "yes, yes, I'm sure... give it to me; I'm so ready." Bobby starts to insert his penis inside of Janey, and she groans; it's a sexy groan indicating slight pain... You want me to stop? No, keep going, just take it slow. Bobby has the entire head of his manhood inside of Janey, and she loves every bit of it, as does Bobby. Now Bobby goes deeper and deeper—until his entire shaft is inside of her, and Bobby lets out a subtle moan, as he says, "Oh my God girl, you are so fucking tight, so wet, and you feel so good. "Bobby is moving back and forth—forth and back enjoying every single stroke, he tries to hold back his orgasm, but it feels so good, and after nine minutes—he too gives in to his orgasm. Bobby collapses on top of Janey, but not before asking, "will you marry me?"

Chapter 15: All Grown Up

So, Janey, tell me, have you considered the conversation we had two weeks ago about your major here at Pennsylvania University? As your academic advisor, it's my duty to ensure you become all that you can be—what core courses are you considering? At the moment, your concentration is general studies; but is there anything you have a passion for? You should consider focusing on a skill while you're in college, get the most out of your education...

Yes, Mrs. McGrier, I'm actually considering psychology; I would like to do more for my community once I graduate. You may have read my admission dissertation. I spoke about the reason I decided to come to college in the first place—and how I initially never saw myself as a college student, but here I am.

Yes, I read your mind-blowing paper, it was amazing, and I'm in awe of your level of maturity and strength. To overcome such a tragedy with flying colors is astonishing.

Thank you, Mrs. McGrier, I appreciate those kind words.

Your welcome, my dear—now let's get you set up with your classes for next semester.

Later that day. Ring-ring-ring...

Mumford "88"

Hello, mother, how are you? I just wanted to give you a call to see how you are doing and to let you know that I switched my major to psychology today. I've been contemplating this decision for quite some time—and I decided that it's a good fit for me. When I receive my degree, I'm going to start a private counseling agency. My concentrating will be children and adolescent trauma. My objective will focus on helping people speak their truth without fear. The practice will be dedicated to the *late,* and if she was alive, *great* Tray X...

Wow, I love it, dear, that's amazing! You're keeping Tray's name going in every way possible, I'm so proud of you, dear...

Thank you, mother, and thanks for always supporting me.

Mom, there is something else I wanted to speak with you about today.

What's that, Janey, what's going on?

It's about Bobby...

Bobby, what about him?

Well, mother, you know we've been dating for a while now—and we never crossed that line, but the relationship is getting heavy. *Janey's mother has 1000 thoughts going through her mind, but she keeps her silence as Janey finishes her statement.* Bobby and I are considering taking our relationship to the next level, and I wanted to touch base with you first—mainly because I would like to start birth control pills. My goal is to complete my degree—and I don't want an unexpected pregnancy to hinder my education. *Janey is no dummy; she did not tell her mother she and Bobby already elevated their relationship to the next level.*

I appreciate your honesty, dear, thanks for telling me, and for coming to me before pregnancy became a reality. You can schedule an appointment with a gynecologist (GYN) and get started on the pill after your next menstrual cycle, but the doctor will give you all the specifications on that. Just remember you must take the pill daily—around the same time...

I will mother, thank you and I must go, my next class starts in an hour...

Okay, Janey. Have a great day, and I will talk to you later.

**** ****

Mumford "88"

A few moments later. Will I marry him, I cannot believe Bobby asked me to marry him. I cannot believe I froze; I was speechless when he asked me that question—he must think I'm so weird. *Janey is talking herself into a frenzy, I better call him, she uttered to herself.*

Hello, Bobby, how are you today? I know it's been a few days since you asked me to marry you, but I needed some time to think. We are both so very young and still very much naive. Also, we are focusing on our education and degree, so I don't think marriage is a good idea—*but,*

Thank God, a *but,* Bobby uttered.

After we complete our studies, it will be my pleasure to be your wife. Please promise me *if* we should marry, we will be together always and forever until death does us part, divorce isn't something I want to encounter. My mother went through hell with my father—divorce was agony for her.

Janey, if you marry me, I guarantee you that I will *never* let you go; you will have to leave me because I will never abandon you.

Honestly, Bobby, I never wanted to marry, but maybe the universe has something different in store for my life. A few years ago, I was mapping out my future to open a clothing boutique after high school—and here I am a stressed-out college student. God is like ha-ha, nope—I have a different path for you, but hey, that's the way the universe works sometimes. So yes, I will marry you, Bobby. You are an amazing boyfriend, and I will be honored to be your wife—once we graduate.

Janey baby, I would marry you tomorrow if you wanted, but I can wait until we complete our education—I think it's a wise choice also. See, this is why I want you to be my wife, you are levelheaded, and sometimes you think too much... but those are the qualities that I adore about you. You are indeed different than many females I know. I will purchase you a promise ring, but we both know it's an engagement ring.

Sounds like a plan, Bobby; we will tell our parents once we graduate.

Okay, but I'll be done the police academy in less than two years; once I find a job, we will tell our parents then, I don't want to wait four years to tell them.

Okay, that sounds fair, Bobby. And once I graduate, with *my* degree, we will set a date to be married—God willing. *They both laughed and sealed the deal with a virtual kiss.*

Mumford "88"

Chapter 16: Not Easy

I'm stressing, Derek. I cannot do this; why did I think I could juggle track practice and my studies. These professors are a pain in my ass; they are so strict, and the grading process is different than general studies. In addition, my coach wants me to be up and out the door before 6 a.m. for aerobics and strength training—five times a week. My first class is at 8:30 a.m.; it's too much, I can't fucking take it no more...

Breathe sis, breathe. You got this, start by taking a deep breath, and know that you can handle whatever life may throw your way, including your professors and coach. So, what's the problem, what caused you to get so worked up, suddenly?
Well, at this moment, my GPA is 3.33; my professors keep giving me B's and C's. The last exam I got a 91, but my professor said anything under a 92 is a B. That's ridiculous; anything in the 90 percent tile should be an A – but apparently, in medical fields, the rules differ. I should have stayed in general studies; it was less intense.

Mumford "88"

Janey, you are a smart girl, you *can* and *will* complete your studies in psychology. Just remember nothing worth having ever come easy...

Oh, I like that saying, Derek, but that statement is easier said than done, but it's a good slogan. Listen up Janey, college, as well as life, can be difficult and overwhelming, don't allow the stressors of life make you believe that you cannot do this college thing. Keep your head up; you got this! You know what you need, lil sis?

What's that, bro, what do I need?

It's the weekend; I'm coming to your campus tomorrow to take you out to relax, you need a night out on the town to unwind. No practice, and no studying for 24 hours, balance is the key you know. Maybe you're burning yourself out.

Wow, you will do that for me, I know your schedule is swamped these days, thank you so much, Derek.

Sure, sis. I'll see you Saturday evening, and Janey, be ready to let your hair down and have some fun, you need and deserve it...

Okay. Thank you again, Derek; I'll see you tomorrow!

You're welcome. That's what big brothers are for, now get some rest, sis.

It's Friday night, and Janey decided to do some reading, but leisure reading. There is a book she was dying to read (Queen Dosma), and tonight was the perfect time to get lost in a book... Saturday morning, Janey worked out than relaxed in the jacuzzi. She had a light lunch and rested until her brother arrived later that evening. "Me time" just what I needed, Janey proclaimed softly to herself. *Note: self-care is a necessity!*

Hey Derek, I'm so happy to see you and thanks again for coming. You look great, big bro, and your outfit looks different; I like! You look like a changed man. What happened to sneakers and straight-up street clothes?

Well, sis, if you must know, I'm getting older, and I had to change my appearance a bit...

Wow, Derek, that's deep and so mature; that's what's up...

Lol, but on the real, Janey, my boo, picked out this outfit for me...

What. Your boo, are you *in love*, Derek?

No, but I have strong feelings for this one, she is kindhearted and smart, and I'm considering introducing her to mom...

Oh, my goodness, Derek, you *do* love her. Why is it that guys will never admit when they are in love with a female? Just say you're in love, it's okay!

Alright, Janey, darn. That's enough... *Derek was blushing and feeling warm and fuzzy inside.*

Derek, since we're sharing, I want to tell you something, but promise you will not tell mom.

What's up, sis, talk to me...

Well, Bobby asked me to marry him four months ago; I said yes, but we're not sharing the good news until after he graduates from the academy.

Wow, Janey, that's amazing. Honestly, I knew he would ask you to be his wife one day; Bobby isn't the player type dude. That day when we saw him in the restaurant, and he came to our house later that evening—his actions said a lot about his intentions for you. I'm happy for you sis; he's going to make a great husband.

Thank you, Derek. I believe Bobby will do right by me too... Okay, enough with the mushy talk, look at us getting sentimental, let's change the subject... Okay, so tonight we are going to have a ball, several parties are happening this evening. You picked a great weekend to come down and show your sister some love. Let's hit the town so I can forget about my troubles.

So, Derek, I guess you won't be hitting on any of the college girls, now that you're *in love*?

I can have fun with them, but I won't sleep with any of them if that's what you are asking.

Aww, look at my brother, he's all grown up, and it looks good on you—keep it up. I'm happy you found a girl who makes you happy and content. I cannot wait to meet her.

****

Later that evening. This band is *hot* tonight, straight-up rock and roll, it's a nice break from R&B and rap music, Derek declared.

Yes, change is good; I listen to alternative genres now. Diversity in music, culture, arts, etc., is essential to growth and development. And here on campus, we are very diverse.

Aww, here you go, dropping your *higher learning* on me...

Mumford "88"

No-no, it's not higher learning; it's the truth, Derek. Multi-cultural experiences are how we advance and learn new things. A person doesn't need a college education to understand that concept. Anyway, let's enjoy the night and see how much mischief we can get into.

Even later that evening. Derek, how about we shoot some pool, those guys just got done playing. I'll rack the balls, and you can get us more drinks, nothing too heavy for me. In fact, I'll take a wine cooler, preferably margarita flavored.

Janey, you are so bossy, but okay, cool, this is your night. But since I'm paying for the drinks, I'm going first, no coin flipping this time...

You got a deal! Janey agrees. *And three games later and three drinks in.... and the crowd is watching and cheering Janey on. She has skills in playing pool, though she is no match for her big brother; after all, he taught her how to play. But Janey makes the game fun and interesting with her excitement and enthusiasm.*

The fourth and final game was amazing, Derek didn't think Janey could get the eight ball into the whole. The 8-ball was positioned in such a way—there was no way an amateur player could make the shot. But luck was on Janey's side tonight, and she aligned her pool stick with the ball and hit the ball at just the right angle and 'voila' just like magic, the ball went into the hole, and the crowd went wild! "Oh!!! Two shots of tequila for the brother and sister duo. You guys rock, that was an awesome game!" *Janey's, feeling tipsy and relaxed; thus, she jumps on top of the pool table and does a sassy and classy swirl, then two other girls join her, and they danced for the crowd for a good two minutes. That was until the bouncer told them to "get their asses down from there!"* What a night, Derek shouted, my sister's a wildcat, she crazy. *It was a night to remember, and the break Janey needed.*

****

I want to thank you, Derek, for coming down here and spending your Saturday night with me, I needed this. By the way, my roommate went home for the weekend, she was stressing about her classes too—I can sleep in her bed, and you can sleep in mine. I don't want you driving home intoxicated, stay here. It's better to be safe than sorry.

Mumford "88"

That sounds great, sis; I'm beat. I'll rest for a few hours, and I'll leave bright and early. I will not wake you if you're still sleeping, but I will leave a note.

Okay, Derek, goodnight, I'm exhausted. *Janey laid her head down, and she was fast asleep.*

A week later. Hey, Sarah, I got an A+ on my exam, things are finally looking up, I had to get over that hump and find my balance, I guess…

Girl, I knew you could do it, we are roommates, and I watched you study your ass off until the wee hours of the morning—then you get up super early for track practice, your determination is admirable.

Thanks, Sarah, and ditto, you're a hard worker too, I'm fortunate to have such an amazing roommate, I lucked out!

Oh, Janey, speaking about roommates, our neighbors across the hall weren't so lucky. They were going at it last weekend, girl; they brought the fight into the hallway in everything! Campus security had to break up the altercation; they were pulling each other's hair, kicking and screaming, it was hilarious. But hey, the fight got them new roommates, so I guess they both are happy now.

I guess so, Janey uttered with a smile. Hey, let's toast sparkling water to good and respectable roommates; we are definitely lucky to have been paired up with one another.

I'll drink to that, Sarah agreed wholeheartedly.

Cheers! *They sipped on flavored water as they played Whitney Houston and Anita Baker's albums throughout the night… It was a Rocking Roommate dorm party.*

Chapter 17: Graduation

That's what I'm talking about; you did it. You completed the Police Academy with no major hiccups, *and* with your scheduled class, you're on a roll. And to top it off, you overcame the cardio challenge; I'm so proud of you, Bobby. Way to go!

Thanks, Babe. I'm ready to join the police force and start getting paid to work; school is out for this cadet. I'm ready to patrol the streets and make a difference in people's lives. And to top it off, I lucked out by getting a full-time job straight out of the academy, who knew I would get hired so fast—and at a local station. God is good!

Oh, yeah. The universe has a way of making things work out—as long as people do their part, situations tend to work out in our favor. You trained and studied your ass off to achieve your position, Bobby; you deserve your title. I have never been so proud of you… *Janey is looking at Bobby, and she's all smiles. She has certainty in her heart that Bobby will make an outstanding police officer.*

Aww, look at Janey smiling; she's all smitten over her man.

Be quiet, Derek, and mind your business; you always have something to say. But yeah, I am happy; in fact, I'm ecstatic for my man! He's going to make a great cop; he's the new and improved *five-0*. He's fresh out of the academy with innovative ideas.

Babe, you're so comical, Bobby replies as he chuckles… Janey, I need to speak with my professor about something, and I need to find my parents, I'm not sure where they went, I'll be back shortly. Just mingle with the crowd; you're good at that!

Okay, Bobby, take your time; I'll be fine. I have Derek to keep me company, and my mom is around here someplace. And this is *your* day; go mingle with your cohorts—take your time.

A few moments later. I thought he'd never leave. Okay everyone listen up, please don't forget to be at my mother's house this evening at 7 p.m., I cannot wait to see the look on Bobby's face when he realizes we threw him a surprise graduation party. Mom, you picked up the chocolate cake for me, right?

Yes, I did, Janey. It's in the refrigerator in the garage; I put it next to the beer and wine coolers.

Okay, great. Bobby loves himself some chocolate cake, thanks, mom…

He sure does, Derek said with a playful tone.

What the heck does that supposed to mean, Derek?

You know, your brown-chocolate and, well—he's white-chocolate; thus, Bobby loves himself some "chocolate cake…"

Lol, I guess it's fair to say, I love myself some "white-chocolate," and it sure is yummy and good to me…

And that's what matters, it must be good too, and for you, it doesn't matter the color of the cake, figuratively speaking…

Yes, mother, we know… We're just having fun; you know how me and Derek get?

Yeah-yeah, I do, but still, behave yourselves. Okay, children, I'm going home to do some last-minute preparations and to wait for the caterers to arrive; I will see everyone later this evening…

Okay, drive safe, mom; I will see you in about 4 hours or so, and thanks again for taking care of the decorations and stuff.

You're welcome, dear, it's my pleasure!

Mumford "88"

Hello, Mr. and Mrs. Hall, did you guys see Bobby? He was looking for you both.

Yes, Janey, we saw our son! He's talking to his professor and a few of his classmates.

Okay, nice... I just wanted to say that I know you both are so proud of him, he worked so hard to complete the academy—he balanced work and school so well, it's commendable.

Yeah. Bobby has made us proud; he's the first police officer in the family. I know he will do positive community policing; that's all he seems to talk about these days...

Yes, Mrs. Hall, he will be an amazing officer; he cannot wait to serve his community and make a difference in the world... If I never said this before, you guys raised an amazing son, he's so generous and caring towards others.

Why, thank you, Janey. We think he's amazing too!

So, Mr. and Mrs. Hall, you remember how to get to my mother's house for the surprise party later this evening, don't you?

Janey, I'm sorry, but I have to stop you here... for the hundredth time, call me Rochelle and my husband, Jarrod? And yeah, we know how to get to your house, we've only been there for dinner at least eight times already, *everyone chuckled.*

Janey, relax, the surprise party will be perfect. Everyone will be on time, and everyone remembers how to get to mom's house.

Thanks, Derek, I just want the evening to be perfect for Bobby's party.

It will go well, sweetheart, and if there are hiccups, we will deal. We are the Halls; nothing goes as planned, but in the end—the results are always spectacular! Later today, I'll tell you the story about my husband's 50th birthday; I'm sure you'll get a kick out of the story.

I cannot wait to hear it. Thanks, Mrs. Hall, I mean momma Rochelle.

Rochelle, honey... Don't you dare tell the story of how I went on my 50th birthday without you—when are you going to get over that situation? Trust me; I've learned my lesson...

Jarrod, dear, I will never forget, and I will never stop telling the story... *The seasoned married couples laughed and giggled as they thought about Jarrod's 50th birthday many years ago... Bobby's graduation was a lovely ceremony; Bobby enjoyed mingling with his fellow graduates, and he had no clue his family was throwing him a surprise party.*

Mumford "88"

****

Later that afternoon. Bobby hurry up, what's taking you so long to get dressed, we're going to be late getting to happy hour at *Melrose Palace*. I'm craving their cocktails; you know they make delicious apple martinis and gin & tonics, right?

Yes, I do babe, I'm almost ready, and I know how you like their drinks... My mind is dragging a little because I cannot believe I'm 21, and I graduated from the Police Academy. The last two years went by so fast; it all feels so surreal. I'm blown away by where I am at in my life; I'm an officer! Can you believe it?

Yes, of course, I can believe it, Bobby! And you're going to do amazing things in the community. I meant what I said when I was talking to Derek earlier today. You have innovative ideas about policing, and you have genuine love for the job; your not in it just for the paycheck...

You're right, babe; ever since I was a kid, I imagined being a police officer, and today is like a dream come true.

Well, alrighty then. Let's get out of this house so we can celebrate your accomplishment....

Okay, let's go! Oh, wait, I forgot something... Janey, go downstairs, I'll be down in a minute. *Janey heads downstairs, and Bobby grabs a surprise for Janey and meets her in the living room.*

Bobby, sometimes you take longer than me to get dressed, but you sure do look and smell good—but we lost an hour, now we'll only have two hours of discounted drinks.

You're so cheap, Janey, but don't worry, drinks are on me, I'm a career man now.

No way, Bobby, I cannot have you paying for our drinks. Derek is meeting use at the tavern; drinks are on him; this is your night!

Oh, Derek's meeting us there? That's what's up! Even better, Bobby asserted. Let's go; I'm ready to celebrate! *Bobby and Janey head out to celebrate the evening at Melrose Palace.*

****

Mumford "88"

Happy hour at Melrose is jamming today; the DJ is playing all my favorite hits, Janey uttered to Bobby... Excuse me, bartender, two gin & tonics, please! *Janey yells across the bar impatiently — she's been craving Melrose cocktails all day... and she's on a secret schedule. The surprise party starts in less than 3 hours.*

Janey, relax, we have all night. Also, I'm not going to have too many drinks tonight; I want to take you to the lake. We always said we would go, but never made time because of our busy class schedules. But tonight, we can just sit still and get lost in the moment...

Okay, wow, that sounds great! But before we head to the lake, I need to stop pass my mother's house, just for a few minutes...

For what, Janey! Darn?

Stop being noisy, Bobby, its girl stuff.

You and your girl stuff; okay, but don't take too long. You know how you and your mom like to talk-talk-talk... I really feel like gazing at the lake this evening; it's a beautiful spring night...

I promise I won't waste time at my mother's house... hey, there is Derek and his girlfriend, Kia.

Derek over here... Bobby waves them down.

Officer Hall, how are you doing, my man?

I'm great! You're looking at the newest police officer with the 17th Police district!

Alright now... don't hurt nothing, Bobby... everyone gave a supportive giggle.

So, Kia girl, how are you doing, Janey asked with excitement in her voice.

I'm fine. I'm happy to be off work this evening. God knows I needed time off; my supervisor has been getting on my nerves lately. How are you, Janey?

I'm great, Kia. My man graduated from the academy today, woohoo!!!

Congratulations, again, Bobby. I'm sure you will clean up the streets in no time!

Thank you kia! I appreciate that.

So, if you see me speeding, you're going to give me a break, Kia said spiritedly?

Nope. No favors from me. I'm going to lock you up and throw away the key... You barely know me, and you have the audacity to ask me for a favor? *Bobby put on a straight face—his expression was as serious as they come. Kia wasn't sure how to respond—and she started to get nervous, then after a few seconds, Bobby, Derek, and Janey started cracking up laughing.* I'm just messing with you, Kia, relax. You know I got you!

Wow, you have a great poker face… you had me scared for a second.
You don't have to be afraid of Bobby… he's an amazing guy, very down to earth. Just be good to him, and he'll be good to you, Janey asserted, before kissing her man on the cheek.

Bobby and Janey, leave Kia alone, you guys are so silly—always playing around… Kia, boo-bear, let's get you a drink and loosen you up a little. Then after, we can play foosball; I know you like that game, what do you say?
Okay, Derek; I'll take a cocktail first, apple martini, please. Then foosball it is!
Everyone sipped on celebratory drinks, then Derek and Kia went to play foosball.
We'll be back guys; I'm going to show Kia how to sock-it to her opponents.
Okay, have fun. Bobby and I will be over in a few; the DJ is jamming tonight. I want to hear the next song and maybe have a quick dance.

A few moments later. Aww, Keith Sweat, that's my jam, you want to dance with me, Bobby?
Umm, sure! I was just thinking the same thing. Let's have a go at it! *Bobby doesn't normally dance to slow songs, but tonight was a special occasion, so he figured, what the heck!*
Sexy ass Keith Sweat; that voice, oh, my God. *Make it Last Forever*, you cannot turn him down on the dance floor, and you know what Bobby, we will definitely make our love last forever, Janey proclaimed in a sexy and seductive tone… *Bobby agreed—and he pulled Janey closer, as he rubbed her backside. And they danced intimately and with deep love and affection.*

Babe, you smell so good, and your skin is so soft; are you wearing a new lotion or something—your scent makes me want to rip your clothes off and devour you…
Mmmm, ripping my clothes off, that sounds good to me… and if we weren't in this pub, I would let you undress me from head to toe… oh, and the aroma is the moisturizer you got me for Valentine's Day, don't you remember?
Oh, yeah, I remember. The sales lady recommended it. She said it was a new arrival.
Well, great buy, Bobby… I'm happy you find the fragrance appealing and sexual—mmmm, what's that I feel? Is that your…. oh, my god, you are so hard. *Then Janey whispers in his ear.* Maybe one day you'll let me taste it...

Taste it!! Wow, Janey, you are so bad. You drive me crazy with your fine ass... *Bobby kisses her on her forehead as he caresses her backside soft and subtly on the dance floor......* He whispers in her ear, "this skirt looks amazing on you, and your ass looks so damn good. I can't wait to get you home; I'm going to tear that ass up!" *Then Bobby takes a handful of her butt and squeezes it. Janey embraces his soft touch and rubs her fingers through his hair; then, she kisses him softly on his neck and lips; then Janey utters,* "I wore this skirt just for you, and I have on a thong; yes, my ass is out." *Bobby visualizes the thong on her butt; thus, he now has a full-blown erection. He has to take a few steps back as his dick is poking Janey's lower belly... They sway on the dance floor as if they're the only two people in the room; the moment is passionate and heartfelt. When the song is over, they linger on the dance floor because Bobby's erection has to subside... Then they engage in a final kiss before they separated to head back to the bar.*

****

Hey, guys, you don't know me, but I saw you two dancing out there, and you guys are one hot ass couple. The love you share radiated in the air. I hope to find genuine love like that one day...
Why thank you, kind stranger, Janey said; I'm sure you will; just give it time, and the right person will come along... *The bystander smiled and walked away with hope.*
She seems like a lovely young lady, Bobby uttered.
Yes, she does. A sweet person like that will certainly find their prince charming.

Janey let's go to the back of the venue to check on Derek and Kia; I bet he's letting Kia win at foosball.
Naw, my brother is very competitive, crazy competitive. There is no way he's letting her win, but come on, let's go; let's see who's winning.
Hey, Kia, girl. Who's winning at foosball? Are you kicking Derek's butt or what?
No! Your brother is winning; he has mad skills. He be like "in your face Kia!" He's lucky he's handsome, and I love his ass. He gets so competitive, but in a teaching kind of way, so I'm not upset. But I long for the day when I finally beat his ass...
Your right about that, Kia; Derek has a love for winning, but he's a great teacher. Derek showed me how to play pool many years ago, and because of his intense teaching practices, I'm good at

it today. And keep at it, I'm sure you'll beat him eventually... Okay, Kia, girl, Derek, and Bobby are looking our way, you better get back to foosball, we'll discuss my crazy brother later.

Later that evening. It's getting crowded in here... I'm ready to go. As you know, I had a long day. I don't want to be around when the twilight crowd arrives... Derek, thank you for the drinks, but Janey and I have someplace else we must be. I want a little peace and quiet with my girl... That's fine, man, I completely understand! Kia and I are going to stay here a little while longer. My friend from high school is a comedian now, and she will hit the stage around 6:30 p.m. I heard she's funny as hell, so I want to stay to support her. I'll see you guys later.

Okay, Derek. That sounds like fun, enjoy, Janey stated. And Derek, don't forget about the meeting next week at 7 p.m., at mommy's house. And don't be late, or mom will be pissed! Okay, Janey, must you always be so bossy, darn... Good luck, Bobby... my sister is a piece of work... *Derek was kidding, of course. Still, Bobby looked at Janey and laughed it off.*

****

Bobby, before we go to my mom's, can we drive past Tray's house? I want to see her house and feel her energy. I have this intense need to go there tonight, will that be okay with you?
Sure, Babe, that will be fine, but I just want to ask, are you okay? Are you feeling well?
Yes, Bobby, I'm fine; why?
Well, you asked to ride past Tray's old house. I want to ensure you don't have a setback. I want to make sure you're not feeling guilty for being happy and successful.
No way, never that. I know that Tray would have wanted me to live my life and to be happy—riding past her house is my way of letting her know that I have not forgotten about her, and I wish she were here; though, I know she's here in spirit...
Yes, she is, Janey. I believe she is here too! Okay, I'll take you past her old house, if that's what you want me to do!
Yes, Please. Thank you, Bobby. *Janey was stalling for time, she called her mother from the payphone at Melrose, and she was aware that the caterer and bartender were running late.*

Mumford "88"

Bobby, give me a few seconds, please. I'm going to step outside of the car and have a moment of silence with Tray. Is that okay with you?
Sure, Babe, go ahead, take your time. *Bobby is unsuspecting that Janey is stalling.*
Outside of the car. Tray, you are still my partner in crime, girl. Thanks for giving me an excuse to stall Bobby so his parents and my mom can finish the last-minute decorations as they wait for the hired help. I want to thank you for being a good friend; I want to thank you for encouraging me to go out with Bobby. I hope you are proud of me, and I wish you were here, but I'm happy you are no longer suffering... I love you, my sister in spirit, Amen... *Janey takes a moment to meditate in the essence of Trays energy before she heads back to the car.*

Okay, I'm ready, Bobby. Let's go. I was having a moment, but I'm better now... You know Ms. Ava sold this house immediately after the funeral. She decided the house held too many bad memories. I admit, selling the home was a great idea. It was a fresh start for Ms. Ava and Beverly. They are finally finding a way to be happy—as they make peace with the fact that Tray is no longer with us.
Janey, once again, I assert that you are a kindhearted woman. I admire the way you keep Tray's memory alive. I love everything about you, and I mean everything, including when you become agitated when you get tired and sleepy... I'm taking the good with the bad, the Yin and the Yang.
Thank you, Bobby, and I love you, too, including when you get bossy with me. You know when you try to police me around, and speak to me in your officer voice?
Ha-ha, I do not police you around, Janey. But sometimes I have to put my foot down—and you're not used to that. You're used to me giving you what you want and spoiling you.
Hmmm. Okay, Bobby, if you say so. But anyway, I know you are firm with me for the right reasons, and you've never steered me wrong, and for that, I appreciate you even more.

Thanks, babe... The sky is getting dark, and it looks like it's about to pour down raining. Let's head to your mother's house, and if it doesn't rain, we can go to the lake. It's funny; I didn't see rain in the forecast for today. The darn weather person is wrong 35% of the time.
I know, right! And okay, I promise I won't be too long at my mom's. And if the rain starts to fall, we can still drive to the lake and watch the rainfall from inside of the car; it will be romantic.
Okay, Janey. Sounds good to me, we will go to the lake – rain or shine.

Mumford "88"

****🍄****

They were sitting at the red-light when Janey noticed Bobby smiling for no reason. What are you smiling about, Bobby? You look so happy and delightful; please share!
Oh, I'm thinking about how we danced to that Keith Sweat song, that was an intense five minutes. I felt like we were the only people in the tavern; I truly got lost in the moment.
Yeah, it was romantic as hell, and the way you whispered in my ear, oh, my God, you know my ear is my spot. And your dick felt so good rubbing against my body; it was hard as fuck! Thinking about it is making me wet...

The light turns green, and it's now pouring down raining. Bobby parks the car in a secluded section underneath a big oak tree, then he states, "I'm impatient, I cannot wait until tonight, I have to kiss your fine ass right now. I feel like I'm going to explode if I don't touch you. Better yet, I want you to climb on my lap and ride me, babe."
Bobby is yearnings for her, and she's yearning for him. Sacred Energy Exchange is in full force... Janey Takes off her seatbelt before leaning in to kiss him—slow, romantic, sensually. Then she follows Bobby's instructions and climbs on top of him—but not before unfastening his belt, unloosing his pants, and taking off her panties... Janey spreads her legs over his body as she slowly and gently inserts Bobby's penis inside her vagina. She's riding him ever so softly, afraid the car will shake if she moves too fast. She kisses him on his lips, the side of his face, neck, then down his chest, and back to his lips. She moves her hips back and forth—and around in a circle—as if she's swooping with a hula-hoop and making that swooshing sound... She exotically whispers in his ear; I'm so proud of you... you did it; you graduated from the academy... *as a moan slips from her lips,* my hero, my officer, my man, my one and only lover, this pussy belongs to you and only you. I love you so much... *At this moment, Janey climaxes; her vajayjay is pulsating and gushes bodily secretions all over Bobby's penis... Bobby says,* Oh, my god, girl... damn, you came a lot, you are so fucking wet, that pussy... fuck!
Bobby is at aww, as this is their first-time making love outside of a bedroom; thus, he releases his warm creamy secretions inside of her as he collapses his head and arms from pure ecstasy... They look into each other's eyes for a little over 30 seconds before separating their bodies and become one.

Mumford "88"

Bobby, we must go back to your house and shower; I cannot see my mother like this; I feel disgusting and dirty; I must get cleaned up, as do you...!
Okay, I was thinking the same thing, put your seatbelt back on, then we will go...

****

You shower first, and I'll shower second, Bobby said... If I get in there with you, I'm going to make love to you all night long. I don't know what's going on, but I'm still hard, I still feel horny. Tonight, when we get home, I'm going to do all sorts of kinky shit to you. So be ready to have multiple orgasms. You're going to be calling my name all night long. I booked a hotel room; I was going to surprise you at the lake, but I'm telling you now—and you can moan and groan as loud as you want, babe...
Mmmm, that sounds good to me, a night to ourselves, yes! I'm kind of aroused myself, still... I feel your cum dripping out of me, and it's making me feel all warm and horney down there.
And at that moment, Bobby takes off his clothes, and Janey sees the passion in his eyes; thus, she takes off her clothes simultaneously. Bobby grabs her by her hair, rough, yet soft—then turns her around, so her ass is facing his dick (doggie style). Then he bends her over on the bed and eases his penis inside of her, and Janey moans a loud moan as cum drips down her leg. Her pussy pulsates over and over again on Bobby's dick, which is at full salute...
Bobby takes his hand and slaps her on her ass several times, and Janey goes wild. The slaps intensify her orgasm, and her pussy oozes warm juicy secretion all over Bobby's dick—it's only been three minutes, and Bobby cannot control his orgasm; thus, he ejaculates yet again inside of Janey. They both say Fuck that was fucking amazing almost concurrently as they gaze off to oblivion... Once they both return to earth, they shower separately and head out the door. It's 7:15 p.m., and Janey is ready to head to her mother's.

Chapter 18: The Party

Where have you been, Janey? It's almost 8 o'clock; you're way behind schedule, my dear. When we spoke on the phone earlier, I said to get here by 7:30, not 8 p.m.

Sorry, mother… Bobby and I saw a few of his classmates, and they started talking about job placement and stuff like that. The next thing I knew, it was pouring down raining, and we had to park under a tree because we couldn't see more than 2 feet in front of us. Then Bobby needed to make an emergency stop at his house, so here we are, late. Please forgive me, mother…

You're forgiven! It's a good thing you were running late, the caterer and bartender didn't arrive until 6:55 p.m. There was an automobile accident on the other end of town, they were stuck in traffic for almost two hours, which delayed their arrival.

Oh, wow! Was anyone seriously injured, mom?

No, thank God. There were a few minor injuries, but no casualties, everyone will survive.

Mumford "88"

A few moments later. Okay, everyone listens up, Bobby is outside in the car waiting on me, after about 10 minutes, he will get agitated and come in looking for me. So, when he enters the foyer, everyone will yell Surprise! Thanks, Janey. I don't think we knew how to yell surprise...!
Shut up, Derek! *Everyone laughs and giggles.*
A few minutes later. Knock-Knock-Knock... *No one answers the door; thus, Bobby enters the house suspenseful.*
Janey, where are you—and why are all the lights off, what the hell is going on? Where is that darn light switch, Bobby mutters to himself. Oh, here it is — *click!*
Surprise!!! *Everyone jumped out of hiding, and Bobby looked surprised and shock, especially when he saw his parents standing way in the back near the kitchen, holding up a banner that read,* "You Did It, Son. We're So Proud of You."

Wow, thank you, everyone! I did not expect a surprise party—aren't surprise parties supposed to be for birthday parties only?
No, Janey proclaimed, a surprise party is for any event, thing, or situation you want to surprise someone for, now enjoy your surprise, Bobby.
Janey, babe; I know this was your idea, wasn't it?
Nope, not entirely, your mom had something to do with it also. *And at that moment, Bobby's favorite cousin Mark came out from hiding, saying,* I can't believe my little big-headed cousin is a police officer, you did it, man, I'm so proud of you, cuz. *Bobby was reasonably shocked—and a tear of gratitude fell from his eye. Then his mother walked up to him and gave him an enormous hug and told him how much she loves him. It was a perfect party; Bobby felt grateful to be surrounded by such love and affection.*

I would like to thank everyone for spending their Saturday evening with me and celebrating my accomplishments; this party was truly a surprise—I had no idea. Janey, you're good at keeping secrets... I want everyone to take comfort in knowing that I will do my best to clean up the streets, positively and optimistically; I will make you all proud, I guarantee you that! And if anyone of you has an issue with parking or speeding tickets... forget my number, e*verybody chuckles.* Naw, but seriously, though, it means the world to me to have everyone here tonight. Mom and Dad, thank you for inviting so many of our family members and close friends to

Mumford "88"

celebrate this day with me. Janey, thank you for inviting so many of your family members to be a part of the celebration—I'm speechless...

Cuz, you're not speechless, you have many words.

Thank you, cousin Mark, for that... *the attendees are laughing and enjoying the humor in the room.*

Where was I before Mark rudely interrupted—oh yeah—this is a very special day, and I could not have planned it better—and I have a surprise of my own... As you all know, Janey and I have been a couple for some time now, and though I was ready to marry her when we entered college, Janey wanted to wait, but now that I have completed my studies, I would like to ask Janey for her hand in marriage. *Bobby walks up to Janey – gets down on one knee, and says,* Janey, I knew I loved you from the moment I saw you—then and there I knew you would be my wife. We had trials and tribulations, but in the end, sincere love overcame all. I know you have a few years left to complete your degree, but will you do me the honor of being my wife? *Janey looks shocked, surprised, and she was for the first time in her life "speechless," especially when Bobby pulled out a sizable diamond ring from his pocket.* It's paid in full; I've been paying for this since I gave you the promise ring your freshman year of college. *There's silence in the room.*

Yes, Bobby, yes! It will be my pleasure to be your wife! *All you heard was Aww and sobs throughout the room; it truly was an evening to remember... Bobby's surprise party will be an event that will be remembered for a lifetime. Everyone danced the evening away as they sipped on cocktails and ate hors d'oeuvres. Janey tried to surprise Bobby, and in return, she too received an unexpected surprise. This is true soul-to-soul harmony!*

Mumford "88"

Chapter 19: Student Leader

It's Homecoming 1994, and Janey has a motivating and uplifting speech prepared for Alumni and current students. Janey was a robust voice for her junior class; thus, she was picked to give the speech at this traditional event... Now a senior, Janey must figure out what her future will hold and how to go about succeeding once she has completed her studies here at Pennsylvania University. One thing is for sure, and that is—Janey loves to speak and help others.

Good evening, student, staff, family, and friends of Pennsylvania University—I am Janey Houston, and I would like to welcome you all to '*Homecoming 1994!*' Woo-Hoo! This semester is going to be just as great as last year—if not, better! We will become smarter, wiser, more intellectual than our previous self. Every year we grow—every day, we become better than who we were yesterday. Focusing on bettering ourselves, never comparing oneself to another, for we are wise enough to know that we are individuals and have intrinsic morals, journeys, majors, hobbies, duties, etc. We reflect on the values of this university, as well as the principles our parents installed in us. Keeping past and current values at heart—as we create standards for ourselves!

Mumford "88"

We will study our butts off, but we will know when a break is required and unwind when needed—as we are doing here tonight. We will treat everyone with dignity and respect, even those whose opinions differ from our own. For we are wise enough to know that every human has innate qualities and relationships with the universe; thus, different goals—can I get an Amen?

Amen, the crowd chants!

We will rejoice! We will dance, eat, and party until the sun comes up! Or until the Dean tells us to get our butts off his campus and go home... *the crowd giggles.* But most importantly, as we celebrate *Homecoming* here tonight, we will keep in mind that we are college professionals and respect our campus and the company that surrounds us... With that being said, who is ready to have a ball, who is ready to party, who is ready to Rock & Roll!!!!!? *The crowd roars, and the fireworks blast in the air, and Janey shouts at the top of her lungs,* Homecoming Beginnings, Pennsylvania University, Class of 1994 make some noise!!!! Woo!!!! *The evening was a blast; everyone enjoyed themselves, there were fire pits everywhere, hot tea & cocoa, hotdogs, burgers, chips, water, soda, music, people, and so much more; it was truly a celebration. Homecoming night was an amazing event—and happy to say that it was an incident-free affair.*

****🎆****

Wow, Janey, Homecoming was great last night, and you did a great job launching the kick-off—that opening speech was so liberating, it was remarkable!

Thanks, Sarah, I'm happy you enjoyed it; but you did help me write the opening speech let's not forget that... Part of my announcement was you speaking up there.

Yeah, that's right, I almost forgot. It was fun writing the speech with you; hopefully, it won't be the last article we write together.

I'm sure it will not, Sarah—we still have the Fall and Spring semesters to conquer. And as I said in the speech, I am looking forward to our final year as undergrads; it's going to be life-changing for us. We'll be graduating with our bachelor's degree, can you believe it, girl?

I sure can, Janey. Honestly, I'm relieved to be almost done. I will not pick up another educational book for an entire year—jeez, college is tough, but good company helped make the years go by faster...

Yes, it did. I had the best company. And I'm looking forward to graduation also. I have several job offers lined up, so many respectable employers to choose from. I had no idea college life would

end with such a successful bang! We are gearing up to cross the finish line, Sarah... keeping in mind that the last quarter sometimes is the hardest, let's make sure to keep motivating and inspiring each other—and come May 1994, we will finally walk across that stage to receive our degree...
I cannot wait! Oh, and congratulations on the job offers, which companies are scouting for you? The Psychiatric Center offered me a full-time position, as well as Mercy Fitzgerald Crisis Center, Belmont Behavior Health, just to name a few.

Wow, that's impressive, Janey. Have you made any decisions yet?
No, not yet. My coach said I have an opportunity to run in the Olympics trials—so I have to decide on that too. But honestly, I want to live *my* life. I have dreams of my own, you know. I always wanted to open my own clothing boutique. *Sexy w/ Class Boutique.* I think it's time to do something for me. But, how can I pass up an opportunity to run in the Olympics trial—it's an opportunity of a lifetime. The Olympics could lead me down a promising path, which could provide enough revenue to start my own business and follow *my* dreams. Besides, Tray would be so proud to have made it all the way to the Olympics—so I must see that through; then I won't have any regrets about my decisions... Life is bewildering; following Tray's dreams could be the key to making my very own dreams come true. The circle of life is astonishing; it's amazing the way situations work themselves out... *The power of positive dialogues; Janey was undecided about her career path, but simply discussing options with her roommate, helped her come to a conclusion about her future endeavors.*
Yes, life is astounding, Janey; Indeed, the universe helps those who help themselves—nothing works out in our favor unless we do our part. And from what I can see, you have done your part.
As did you, Sarah, and well said. Thank you so much for always being a listening ear and for always motivating me. I could not have done any of this without you!
I feel the same way, Janey, so I guess we both are grateful for one another.
I agree; we are!

****

Bobby's a working man, and he's getting used to his new career. He's learning how to navigate through the ups and downs of the police force.
Ring-Ring-Ring... Hey, Janey, how are you doing? And my apologies for the late phone call, but I'm having a stressful day at work.

Mumford "88"

Stressful, why, what happened, and are you okay?
Yeah, I'm fine, babe. I answered a domestic violence call today, and it got under my skin, it bothered me a little, that's all.
Oh, okay… well, what happened—can you share a few details about the incident?
Yeah, I can discuss a few details with you, babe… In a nutshell, it was a family quarrel. The husband came home late from work and started beating on his wife. Regrettable, the children were witness to the incident—and that did not sit well with me… *Bobby experienced a repressed flashback from his younger years. Unfortunately, Bobby witnesses his uncle beating on his girlfriend many years ago, which lead to the cops being called to the scene. That very incident is the reason Bobby decided to become a police officer…* I just don't understand why people expose their children to cowardly acts of violence. And to add insult to injury, the jerk damn near admitted that he was cheating on his wife. It seemed as though he felt it was okay to have other women. He sickened me.

Wow, double heartache; domestic violence *and* a broken heart, Janey uttered…
Yeah, I know. I got the call around 10 p.m., the wife said the husband never came home from work, he claimed he had someplace to be after he got off but didn't say where. The wife was not happy with his disappearing act. The family was planning a road trip to Virginia in the morning; the wife was upset because *she* took the car to the shop to make sure it was ready for the road, she packed the children's bags, purchased the gift for her husband's military buddy, etc. Basically, she handled the business while her husband was out cheating. When he came home this evening, the wife was furious; I guess she had enough. Words got heated, and he smacked her around a couple of times. The older sibling called 911—asking the cops to come and help her mommy.
It's frustrating to see people treat their families with such disrespect and lack of care. And to make the situation worse, he was nonchalant about the status quo; he didn't show one ounce of care towards his family. The husband actually stated, "well, I pay all the bills, who is she to question what I do." Out of agitation, I said, she's your wife—that's who the hell she is; thus, deserves respect. She's also the mother of your children; you don't think that position deserves respect? And Janey, the idiot said, "No, she doesn't do anything all day; her job is easy, why should I respect her." The guy is an egotistic prick.

Mumford "88"

Oh, wow. It sounds to me like the husband has some control issues and is a bit of a womanizer, maybe even a little narcissistic to a certain extent.
Yes, babe, I agree. Did you just social analyze him based on the information I gave you?
Yes, I did Bobby, occupational hazard, sorry.

Anyways, I gave the wife your number; hopefully, she will call you for an initial session. I was telling her how you focus on mindfulness-based stress reduction and awareness exercises—helping people realize when they're in toxic situations and helping them stand on their own two feet. Maybe she can benefit from your practices; I would like to see her become a provider for her children. Then she won't need to depend on her idiot husband to pay the bills or buy food, clothing, etc., for the children
.

Bobby, you have an amazing heart—I love how you took the time to discuss the situation with the wife—I hope she calls me too. I know a few people in the domestic relations department, and they can help her build independence if financial stability is what she wants; they can also assist with spousal and child support. The support payments can pay the bills while the wife seeks employment, develop a trade/skill, etc. And I will work on rebuilding her spirits and mental strength—which is often stripped away when people experience mental and/or physical abuse...
You are so resourceful. I'm sure you can assist her—if she wants help, that is. I had a short conversation with her, and I don't know if she's ready to leave him, but time will tell. I also spoke briefly with the husband, but I couldn't talk to him for long; his words irritated my soul. My partner completed his statement, and I went back to speak with the wife and kids, mainly because I wanted to give her your information.

In the end, we asked the husband to leave home, just for the night—he was talking some off the wall shit my partner said; maybe he was high on something, nobody in their right mind thinks that way. I gave him a fair warning, informing him that distance is needed when ill feelings are in the air, and people don't see eye-to-eye. Honestly, I was afraid he would harm his family after we left, but the wife didn't want to press charges, and I didn't want to lock him up—they are such a young couple. However, I told them both that I will personally return to arrest him if

Mumford "88"

another domestic violence call is made from their address. Those children don't need to experience violence at such a young age.

 That is correct, Bobby, but kids don't need to see violence at all. Especially coming from their parents—they are supposed to love and care for one another, not cause physical and emotional harm to each other.

You did great, Bobby... you gave the husband a break. And you are correct—I can hear the tension in your voice; the situation did get to you... Remember, we both agreed that we would not allow our work to get under our skin. We both will be exposed to heartbreaking situations, but we mustn't take work personally. You did the right thing, and I hope the wife calls me for assistance, but if she doesn't, there is nothing we can do. And if she takes her husband back, that too is out of our hands. I will keep an ear out for her call—what's her name?

Oh, her name is Tina... Hold on; dispatch is on the radio, I'll call you back in a few.

Dispatch, this is officer Hall, is this regarding another 10-16?

It is... That domestic violence stop you were on earlier, made another 911 call. The caller said her husband returned, and he's disturbing the peace. Do you and officer Asher want to return to the scene? I know your shift is almost over.

Yes. Absolutely, we'll head to the site. I want to be the arresting officer, thank you dispatch. *Bobby and Asher speed to the residence...*

A few minutes later... Knock-Kock-knock. What seems to be the problem, ma'am? *Then Bobby looks at Tina's face and realizes she is bruised, and her lip is bleeding; she now has visible injuries, an arrest must be made. Tina still doesn't want to press charges, but Bobby is unrelenting and arrest the husband, anyway.* You have the right to remain silent, anything you say can and will be used against you in a court of law; you have a right to an attorney, If you cannot afford one, "you prick" one will be appointed to you. *Tina is crying and pleads with the officers to please don't arrest her husband. The police officers know better and will not give the husband another chance; thus, they take him away in handcuffs; regrettably, the children witness everything.*

Mumford "88"

As they drive to the police station, Bobby has an in-depth conversation with the husband. Josh, I hope you get the help you need as you endure pending charges and repeated court dates, but you brought this on yourself. You have a lovely wife and beautiful children. Love them the way you want to be loved, treat them the way you expect to be treated. Don't ruin your children's life and childhood with violent memories, give them more than what was offered to you. Show them a happy home, show them how a man must love a woman… If you want my help, I will assist you, but a Protection from Abuse Order (PFA) will be in effect, now you *won't* be able to return to your home until the order is vacated. I warned you what would happen if another domestic violence call was made from your address. This arrest is the consequence of *your* actions. Let's just hope the children aren't permanently affected by the violent behavior towards their mother.

Officer Hall, I hear you loud and clearly, Josh declares, but may I add—my father beat my mother every so often—and their relationship was perfect. Men hit women but not enough to cause serious bodily harm; this is the way of the world…
I'm sorry you feel that way, Josh, but that perception of a loving family is not correct. So that you know, I'm recommending counseling based on the statement you just made. In all fairness, plead the 5th and keep your mouth shut, don't dig your hole even deeper.

Later that evening. Ring-Ring-Ring… Hey, it's Bobby; are you awake? Sorry I hung up the phone so fast, but you know how it is, I was still on duty…
What… what time is it? *Janey is in dreamland; it's the wee hours of the morning, are you okay?*
Yeah, I'm fine. It's 1:55 a.m., I reverted to that domestic violence call, the husband returned home, and he used his wife's face as a punching bag; now he's behind bars where he belongs. I'm about to shower and get some rest; I'm beat, this shift was long. I just wanted to call to let you know that I'm home and to say goodnight, babe…
Okay, Bobby, I'm happy your safe; goodnight and rest up, I'll talk to you in the morning. Love you, I can't keep my eyes open. *Janey hangs up the phone and falls back to sleep.*

Chapter 20: Revelations

Mom, the wedding is one month away, and I graduate in less than two weeks—I cannot believe how time flies. I'm about to graduate from college; I cannot believe it. I did it; I pulled it off...!
Yes, you did, Janey, and you have made me very proud. The way you kept Tray's dream alive during your entire journey is commendable, noble, and highly respectable...
Aww, thanks, mom—and mom, please don't throw me a graduation party, the wedding is my main concern. Let's have an intimate family dinner and call it a day. I will party and jam during the wedding reception; it will be a two-for-one deal for me!
Okay, dear, I heard you loud and clear the first five times; I will not throw you a graduation party; I promise you that. I think your reasons are valid and fair. Why throw two big parties so close together. You're savvy with your time and money, that's a good thing.

Thanks. By the way, I decided to turn down the job offers and run track in the Olympics. It was a hard decision, and I dwelled on it for months, but I feel the Olympics is the way to go. It just makes sense to be associated with a prestigious organization. The recognition alone will be beneficial once my private practice is up and running.

Honestly, Janey, choosing to work for a large company or running in the Olympics are both esteemed options—you cannot go wrong with either decision. But I'm happy that you are following your heart and not the immediate money.

Thanks, mom, I figured I would open my boutique and start a private practice after I complete the final chapter of Tray's dream. I must admit, I'm looking forward to practicing psychology. I have fallen in love with mental health and mindfulness studies. I enjoy helping people focus on discovering ways to find their inner peace and solitude within—as they change their behavior patterns for the better. Of course, everyone won't make changes for the best, but many people will. I realize that everyone doesn't want happiness and/or serenity; they prefer their comfort zone, no matter how unstable or unhappy the situation may be.

I'm so thankful that I switched my major from general studies and selected and actual skill to study. I'm happy to say that I've learned a great deal during my time as a college student and have developed incredible building blocks to assist future patients in trauma, domestics relations, family counseling, drug addiction, and so much more. But honestly, mother, textbook learning gave me the foundation, but I must use life experiences and common sense when helping someone find their way in life. I've been thinking about this for quite some time; I'm calling my approach Interpersonal Therapy Counseling. Thus, I won't always follow textbook methods. Indeed, helping people who are experiencing a personal crisis, need creative and innovative counseling which isn't always found in a textbook because it's interpersonal—individualized for each individual. I will help them find *their* happiness, *their* way—understanding that we all heal differently, hence, interpersonal counseling.

Spoken like a seasoned mental health professional, you are ready to face the world. Pennsylvania University has taught you well.

Yes, they have, and I will eventually practice, but I feel as though I'm not ready to be a therapist. I believe running in the Olympics will broaden my understanding of life and add to my professional experiences and development. Thus, when I finally open my counseling agency, I will be a seasoned and experienced adult... Mother, I appreciate your support and kind words. You're a great role model and the reason I am who I am today.

Thank you, dear. And you're an amazing daughter, a fantastic sister, and an incredible friend; you and your brother both have made me a very proud parent, I see a prosperous future for you both. Keep up the good work, my dear... I'm sure Tray's love and grace are shining down on you.

Thanks, mother, I hope so... *Janey and her mother have a moment of silence as they embrace each other's words of affirmation, love, and support.*

**** ****

Chapter 21; The Wedding

The wedding day. Today is Sunday, August 8th the sun is shining, and the birds are chirping. It's a joyous and blessed day to unite such a beautiful couple. When Bobby and Janey asked me to perform their wedding ceremony, I was delighted and honored. I've known these two for quite some time—and to know them, I cannot help but recognize the love and respect they share for one another. To find a sincere bond is what many people are searching for. Indeed, when people are touched by God, they aspire to live a peaceful and happy lifestyle—gravitating towards an existence and behavior patterns that are pleasing to the universe; thus, bringing abundance, stability, and happiness to their life. I think we all can agree when a person finds a spouse; they have found a wonderful thing. Can I get an Amen?
Amen, the crowd says in agreeance.
Do you Bobby, take Janey, to be your lawfully wedded wife, to have and to hold in sickness and in health, for richer or for poor for as long as you both shall live?
I do.

Do you, Janey, take Bobby, to be your lawfully wedded husband, to have and to hold in sickness and in health, for richer or for poor—for as long as you both shall live?
I do.
Is there anyone here who knows why these two shall not be married? If so, it is too late, and may you forever hold your peace. By the power vested in me and by the state of Pennsylvania, I now pronounce you husband and wife. You may kiss your beautiful bride. *The attendees roar "Awwww," as Bobby and Janey engage in a brief, respectable kiss...*

****💍****

Later that day. Realization sinks in. I cannot believe we're married. Bobby. We did it! We tied-the-knot! I feel so happy, so lucky in love... Wake me up, am I dreaming...?
You are very much awake, and we are very much in love. Yes, we did it; you are my wife, my partner for life. I must admit, I'm happy you wanted to wait until now to marry. Over the last few years, I have grown and developed a better understanding of what it means to be a man. If we had married our freshmen year of college, I would have been still learning how to be a provider for my wife, though I'm sure I would have succeeded, it just would have been harder... Today I feel like the luckiest man alive; I've never been happier, thanks for becoming my wife.

Wow, you're amazing, I appreciate you so much... you have made *me* the luckiest woman in the world by simply being you, a sincere gentleman, a perfect boyfriend, and, most importantly, a positive influence in my life. Never have you tried to change my ways or talked me out of an idea... I love how you support my decisions, even if you do not agree with them, that means the world to me. Indeed, true love offers freedom, not control... I'm putting my counselor's hat on with this statement—because it is true, but one doesn't need a degree to realize that fact! *They both smile as they gaze into each other's eyes—embracing the moment.*

****♥****

A few moments later. Can you believe the turnout here today? I think everyone who RSVP came out to support us—we are truly blessed to have supportive family and friends.
Yes, we are, Janey, and speaking of supportive, did you see the gift table? There are so many presents, so many envelopes—we racked up, babe.

Mumford "88"

Yeah, we did! We racked up big time. I cannot wait to see what gift was purchased from our registry; there were a lot of home goods to choose from; we better buy a house soon; these gifts will take up half my mother's garage... We will have to mail out a lot of thank you cards too, I purchased a few boxes already, so we can fill them out as we are opening gifts. I want to thank the attendees for the gifts we received personally. I don't want to send a general thank you response, that's so impersonal... *Bobby was looking at Janey affectionately and with an enormous smile on his face. Then and there, he reaffirmed himself that he made the right decision, though affirmation wasn't needed...*
I know you wouldn't have it any other way. You have style and class—you want our guests to know that their gifts were received and appreciated, and I love that about you.
Thanks, Bobby; that makes me feel warm and fuzzy inside, Janey proclaimed playfully.

Oh, and speaking of wedding gifts, I have something special for you, Bobby. It's a private gift; we will have to go to the honeymoon suite if you want to unwrap your surprise. I've been anticipating this day for a while—and now that I'm your wife, I do not have to hold back any longer...
Really, what's going on inside that beautiful mind of yours? Are you ovulating or something, you want to make a baby right away?
No way, are you crazy—we are not ready for that! I'm staying on birth control pills; I do not see babies in our near future. I want to live for us; I want to enjoy the honeymoon years of our marriage before we bring life into this world. Let's indulge in one another; then, we'll expand our love to a baby.
Fair enough, Janey, but just so you know, I'm ready to start a family. Though I had a feeling you would say you weren't ready—and I respect and appreciate your wishes, but in the meantime, we will have fun practicing.
Sounds good to me, Bobby. And your surprise gift is in alliance with practicing...
Oh really, Bobby said with amusement and anticipation. Now I'm really looking forward to my surprise gift, babe.
And I promise you; it *is* something to look forward too. It will bring you satisfaction and great pleasure. I'm sure of it.
Mmmmm, Bobby uttered tenderly and handsomely.

Mumford "88"

Janey paused, then said, Bobby, come closer, I want to share something with you... I'm craving something hard and sweet.
What are you craving, babe? Your wish is my command!
I'm craving a lollipop... can you be mine? I want to taste and suck your lollipop all night long. My mouth has been yearning and watering to taste your manhood for quite some time. I'm ready —I want to feel you explode in my mouth. I want to pleasure you with my tongue, lips, saliva, my entire mouth, Ummm, I can taste you already...

Wait. You want what now? Oh, my goodness, girl, you have such a potty-mouth, and in your wedding gown, you're so bad; you're supposed to be a lady, Bobby uttered with pleasure...
I've been having filthy thoughts for over a week now; it must be the wedding *and* the fact that we took an oath to restrain from sex until after the wedding... But the wedding is over, and I'm telling you that I'm horny; we didn't make love in over a month! I'm going to devour you...
Janey leans in closer to Bobby—she moans, then says, every man wants a lady in the street but a freak in the bed, and you know I got both fields covered!
That, you do... you're my strong, sophisticated, educated, sexy ass wife, the women of my dreams.
Aww, Janey utters.
And babe, I know every woman wants a dependable, faithful husband, who knows how to make his wife smile, have multiple orgasms, and can protect her to the very end. Do I fit the bill, wifey?
Yes, you do, hubby. You're definitely a resilient protector, which often gets me hot and bothered. I love your firmness; it's sexy as hell. See now I'm imagining you fucking me in tonight!

Janey, shh! Your extremely naughty today. What has gotten into you?
It's what hasn't gotten into me, but I'm sure that issue will be resolved very soon.
Shh! I think the photographer is coming our way once she's done taking pictures of the wedding cake—she just signaled me. So shh, babe, be quiet. You're getting my dick hard...
Okay, I can code-switch at the drop of a dime... Our three-tiered wedding cake sure is beautiful, and wait until you taste it, the cake samples were delicious... Once the photographer is done

taking pictures—lets head to the honeymoon suite so I can take off this hot ass wedding gown and put on something a little more comfortable. And maybe we can have a quickie before we return to the reception hall? I need something to take the edge off!

Okay, babe, your own! I'm going to tear that pussy up. I'm going to tease you first. I'm going to lick and suck on your dark, luscious nipples; then enter your pussy nice and slow. So make sure your body is wet and ready for me.

Done! Janey acknowledges with a smirk!

The photographer is headed their way and interrupts Bobby and Janey's erotic conversation; thus, there is simmering sexual tension between the two during their final photoshoot. As a result, the images were smoking hot... Thankfully, the wedding party didn't pick up the vibes that were I the air.

Everyone, please come together to take final pictures. Can the bride and groom situate yourself in the middle, parents stand by your child's side, and the rest of the wedding party stand on the opposite end—bridesmaids stand together, and groomsmen stand side by side; now everybody smile and say, "Happy wife, happy life."

Happy wife, happy life, everyone chants!

Dam straight, Bobby utters, and everyone laughs.

Thank you so much, you are a great photographer, and I love the way you directed and told us where and how to stand, you're a true professional. We will definitely send referrals your way. If possible, can you hang around for the reception and take additional pictures. We will pay you overtime, plus a bonus...

Yes! Absolutely. And thank you, Janey, and congratulations again to you and the groom. *The photographer was low on cash and staying longer; hence increasing her income for the day was precisely what she was hoping... Once again, you do your part, and the universe makes a way!*

Bobby is hot and bothered. Okay, everybody, listen up. My wife and I are going to change into something a little more comfortable. Please enjoy each other's company and be nice to one another. Don't make me have to arrest anyone, *the attendee's chuckle...* They're serving cocktails in the far-left corner, and the hostess will be walking around the room with appetizers, so eat up! We will join the reception within the hour.

****

The honeymoon suite. You truly are a magnificent bride; you look like an angel in your champagne colored wedding gown, I have no doubt in my mind that I married the women of my dreams. You're all I want and will ever need. You got me hooked; I'm whipped, girl...
You are such a gentleman, Bobby; I love you. And you look handsome in your Italian slim cut tuxedo. Come closer, let me hug you, and embrace my husband's sexy ass body... Oh, my god, Bobby, you feel so damn good! I love your muscular physique... *Janey embraces Bobby with an erotic hug.* Oh, I feel your manhood rising; I love how fast your dick gets hard for me... *Janey caresses Bobby's chest, arms, neck, face, and hair; she's enjoying her husband every muscle, then Janey whispers in a sexy tone,* Now let me help you get out of this suit, I want your dick inside of my mouth, right now. *Janey moans then says;* my body is aching for your dick; are you ready for me to put that big-thick penis in my mouth? I want to taste it so bad.

Come here, Mrs. Hall, your erotica is on fire tonight, why are you so bad? But I must admit, I love it—you drive me crazy—that mouth of yours is so sexy. *Then Bobby proceeds to kiss Janey softly and passionately on her lips. Janey, knees buckle, she is yearning for her husband, her vagina is soaking wet, but Bobby delays and gives a final speech, which further intensified Janey's horniness.*
Before we go any further, Janey, I want you to know that my goal is to make you the happiest woman on the face of this earth, I will protect and love you the way you deserve to be loved—I will put you first and ensure you want for nothing. You are my match, my soulmate, and now my wife—I love you, Janey M. Houston-Hall. Always and forever.

Janey's sexual excitement eases, as she feels the love and respect in the atmosphere that is generating from her husband; thus, a tear of gratitude falls from her eye. She hugs and kisses Bobby ever so gently and says, thank you for loving me the way that you do and for putting up with my craziness. *Then Bobby takes off her Tierra, then unzips her gown, and gently lays it on the chaise. Bobby removes all her clothing, all except the garter and the garter belt. He kisses her body from front to back, and spends a little extra time caressing her breast and nipples...*

Then he says, I will love you forever, I will love you for always, and your body is so fucking hot, god-damn! *Janey Giggles… He then caresses her legs and kisses her inner thighs and slowly moves downwards towards her toes, Janey utters softly* that tickles Bobby, what are you doing? I'm loving every bit of your body, babe. Just relax and enjoy my tender kisses. *Janey moans and groans as Bobby appreciates every angle of her body. Then Janey whispers,* we have to get moving—we have to get showered and dressed—then head to the reception; but before we go… *then Janey repositions herself on top of Bobby and strokes his penis with her hand, she had some baby oil on the table and used that to get a warm and smooth motion going.* That feels so good. Damn Janey, you're a pro, don't stop.

Oh, I'm just getting started. Close your eyes… just relax. I'm about to give you your wedding present. *Once Janey's strokes have dissolved all the baby oil from her husband's penis—Janey kisses his chest, six-pack abs, and finally his dick. She opens her mouth wide and embraces his penis—her mouth is already watering with anticipation, and she releases a sexy sigh. Janey wanted to taste Bobby's penis since the night she lost her virginity… Bobby jumps, he's surprised, and his dick is extra hard (standing in full attention). Bobby is excited, and he precums, and Janey says,* Oh, my god, you taste so delicious, your cum is so warm and creamy inside my mouth. *Bobby moans and says,* Damn, girl, you got made skills; fuck, you're really good. *Janey is sucking and licking on his dick like it's a Bomb Pop, she's moving her head left and right—up and down—making sexy slurping sounds—as if it's the best Bomb Pop she ever tasted. She's using her hand to stroke his penis—up and down—around and around her hand goes—almost simultaneously with her sucks…. Bobby's penis is in shock; it never experienced anything like this before; thus, he unexpectantly explodes in Janey's mouth.*

Fuck, Janey, that was good as fuck, damn. I'm so sorry I didn't warn you I was about to cum, but I couldn't talk for a few seconds… you got me sprung, girl…. *Janey whispers,* and you know what, that felt so got damn good in my mouth. I never mentioned this before, but when I was younger, I used to suck my thumb—but sucking your dick is even better…
What, oh my god girl—you have such a sexy-ass potty mouth—what am I going to do with you?

Mumford "88"

You're going to fuck me and continue to love me. And this potty mouth, this body, these words are only for you, my husband. No one else will ever see this side of me; this is exclusively for you, remember that!

I know, babe!

Bobby and Janey snuggle for a few minutes, both feeling contentment about their life together; then they take a quick shower—which leads to a quickie in the shower... Finally, they are dressed to impress and ready for the second half of the evening.

Mumford "88"

Chapter 22: The Reception

Ladies in Gentlemen, may I have your attention, *as Stephanie Mills "I Never Knew Love like this Before" plays subtly in the background...* Introducing for the very first time, Mr. and Mrs. Bobby Hall. *Everyone stands and claps—as Janey and Bobby enters the room and entertain their guest as they dance and spin on the dance floor before walking up to the microphone and saying a few words... and yes, Janey's prepared a brief speech.* Thank you for the introduction, DJ Blue—I would like to thank you all for celebrating this special day with my husband and I. Husband, that sounds funny Janey utters—and the guest chuckles. It means the world to us to have you all here today. Because of you, our wedding day will be a day to remember—your attendance fills the space in this oversized reception hall. Celebrating this special day with us allows our wedding day to linger longer. Indeed, heaps of people make an event such as this memorable. So, thank you all, and thank you for the amazing gifts. The gift table is filled to capacity, we genuinely feel blessed, and we are genuinely grateful.

I agree with my wife 100%, and I too thank everyone for spending your Sunday evening with Janey and me, we love and appreciate you all. We hope everyone is enjoying the hors d'oeuvres; dinner will be served shortly. And yes, it's an open bar, but please drink responsibly, we want everyone to make it home safe and sound...

I'll drink to that, Mark asserted.

Of course, you will, Bobby said jokingly—you'll drink to anything Cousin Mark, *the attendees are humored, they are enjoying the music and good company as they prepare for the main course meal.*

****

A couple hours later. Hello, Janey, darling, how are you holding up on your big day? I cannot help but stare. You and Bobby look so adorable together, I'm so proud of you, sweetheart. You have chosen a wonderful husband; I have no doubt in my mind that you and Bobby will have a joyful life together; I am satisfied with your choice.

Thanks, mom, I'm holding up well, and I agree, Bobby is an amazing man, and I'm so looking forward to my future with him. I knew from the start that Bobby was the type of guy you would be okay with me marrying. I considered your judgment when choosing him as a boyfriend. Your opinion means everything to me, mother.

Thank you, Janey, I appreciate that vote of trust.

Of course, mother… Oh, I'm sorry to cut this conversation short, but if you would excuse me for a second, I have to use the restroom; I had one too many cups of water.

Sure, Janey, go ahead... Do you need my help in the bathroom? The train on your reception dress is just as long as the train on your oversized wedding gown.

Oh, my goodness, mother, yes; help would be great, thank you!

A few moments later… My bladder is relieved; I feel much better now. Thanks, mother, for helping me in the bathroom. It's been over a decade since I needed help from my mother in the lavatory; life has truly come full circle. Thinking of full circle, I remember when I was a kid,

Mumford "88"

every Sunday was "Salmon Sunday" *Janey and her mother recited simultaneously.* Derek and I used to love Sunday dinners. Well, we still do, but we no longer have Salmon Sundays. Now it's whatever meat is on sale Sundays. Today it's more like "Sale Sunday," but I'm not complaining mother. I'm just thankful to be able to have Sunday dinners with my family.
I know you are appreciative, dear; I've raised you to be grateful.
Yes, you did, mother, you sure did.

But speaking of Salmon Sundays, the salmon was delicious this evening. It wasn't overcooked, and it was seasoned just right—and the asparagus was sautéed precisely the way I like it, kudos to the chef, she put her heart into preparing the meal for your wedding...
Thank you, mom, Bobby, picked the meal—and he had no idea about Salmon Sundays, it's coincidental, and a sign that he's meant to be in our life...
I agree, Bobby fit in right from the start, and he and Derek had a bond from the beginning, and you know your brother is picking when it comes to his circle of trusted friends...
Yes, I do mom, Derek is funny like that, but he's a "ride or die," type of guy—a friend to the end. In fact, I'm pretty sure Bobby and Derek knew each other way before I came into the picture.
I think you are correct, dear. Anyhow, where is your husband? I've been trying to talk to him all night; I think he's avoiding the mother and son-in-law talk.
Mom, you're too funny... Bobby went outside to speak to his parents. His mom is getting tired; she isn't feeling well, actually. They will be headed home soon.
Oh okay. I hope she's okay. Though I'm sure Bobby will guarantee his parent's safety, he's responsible like that! So, before your husband gets back from taking care of his parents, can I have a dance with my beautiful daughter?
Of course, you can, mother, it will be my pleasure. *The DJ realizes Janey and her mom are dancing, and he plays "The Spinners—Sadie."*

****

Thanks for the dance mom, you were jamming, you still got moves—and what a beautiful song the DJ played for us. *Sadie* will forever be embedded in my brain.

Mumford "88"

Yes. The DJ is observant and very good at what he does. And you are correct, every time I hear *Sadie* I will think of this day, this moment here with you... Your wedding truly is a beautiful event; you and Bobby hired the right people to ensure this day turned out perfectly... And Janey, I might be getting older, but I can still get down on the dance floor, remember that, young buck! Mom, you're hilarious this evening, I feel like this is what having a big sister would have been like. This reminds me of the times when I was younger, and you, me, and Derek would watch horror flicks and eat popcorn all night long, you truly are a good mom. I love you, always and forever... Oh, speaking of Derek, there he is. I'm going to talk to him; I feel like I haven't seen him all night.

Okay, dear, I'm going to get a glass of red wine; I'm feeling relaxed and jubilant. If you need me, you can find me on the terrace, and when you see your husband, please tell him to find me. Okay, mother, I will.

Hey Derek, what's going on, where have you been? I feel like I haven't seen you all night.
Hey, sis, what are you talking about, I've been here all day; I was holding down the spot when you and Bobby were getting changed. Then Kia got sick, and I took her home, it was heavy traffic getting back over this end, so I was missing in action for a while.
Oh, my, is Kia, okay? Bobby's mother didn't feel well either; I hope it wasn't the food.
No, the meal was delicious sis—and Kia will be fine, *Derek pauses for a few seconds*... Kia and I are expecting a baby, it wasn't planned, but I'm excited about the pregnancy.
What... say what now—oh my goodness, Derek; you're going to be a father?
Yes, I am—and you're going to be an aunt...
I cannot believe this; I'm so excited for you, does mom know?
No, mom doesn't know... Kia and I wanted to wait until after your wedding to tell mom.
Wow, mommy is going to be so happy, her first grandchild. God knows I'm not having kids anytime soon. I cannot win the Olympics pregnant.
Ha-ha, no, you cannot sis, no you cannot. But on the real, I want to say congratulations to you on all your many accomplishments, I brag about you often, and Bobby is a lucky guy...
Thanks, bro, I appreciate you and how you always have my back, no matter what. I'm fortunate to have an amazing brother and now an amazing husband; sometimes, I cannot believe my luck.

Mumford "88"

Your welcome, sis. You're a wonderful person. I'm happy your life is going well, despite adversities along the way; your perseverance is admirable. Now give your brother and hug. *Janey and Derek hug it out, and Janey congratulates her brother one more time on the conception of his first child.*

****🕊****

The couple's official dance. Everyone listen up, this is DJ Blue, and it is obvious that everyone here is having a great time, but I'm going to have to ask everyone to please leave the dance floor for about 5-10 minutes. The bride and groom are going to have their first slow dance as husband and wife. Note; I cannot say *first dance* because the two were already on the dance floor dancing the night away. But Mrs. Hall asked me to play *Saving all my Love, By Whitney Houston*—and Janey wanted me to say, and I quote her on this, "because I saved all my love for my husband." Aww, the attendees uttered... *The two dances slowly and with deep love as their guest watches with well-wishes and happy thoughts.*

****

Later that evening... My goodness, Bobby, this was an amazing day. We are going to need help getting all these presents to my mom's house. Oh, and Bobby, the wedding card box with all the cash, bring that to the honeymoon suite, I want to count it up tonight. I'm anxious to know how much money is inside of it... Maybe we can look for a house to rent after we return from our honeymoon; we'll need someplace to layout our wedding gifts.

Bobby pauses for a second. Okay, Janey. I'm on it... It's getting late anyway; I'll take the box up to the room. It will be waiting for *you* because I'm not counting anything tonight, I'm too tired...

Thanks, Bobby. The last guests are getting ready to leave, so we can finally call it a night. I didn't think people would hang around for as long as they did, I'm shocked.

Janey, your funny; the food was good; the DJ was jamming, and the drinks were free, I knew it would last long—except for my parents, my mom got sick unexpectedly.

Yes, she told me, and she expressed regret for leaving so soon. Make sure we call your parents first thing in the morning to check on them.

Absolutely.

Mumford "88"

Oh, Bobby, guess what! Derek and Kia are expecting a baby; that's why she had to leave so suddenly! Apparently, she gets morning sickness during the evening.
Wow, so Derek's going to be a father, good for him!
Yeah, I know, I'm excited to be an aunt and you an uncle. This is good news, my mom will be so happy, and I get to spoil a baby. Life is good; we are not children anymore; we are adults. We have reached new chapters in our lives, and I'm excited to see how the story will read.
Yes, Janey, we are entering new chapters of our lives, adulthood—when did that happen, and how do we make it stop?
What, excuse me, Bobby?
I'm just playing babe; I love you so much, and I'm happy we get to spend the rest of our life together. I'm proud to be a responsible adult, and I take pride in knowing that I will be a great husband to you. Together we can accomplish anything, and together we will… *Janey and Bobby engage in a brief kiss before seeing their last guest off for the evening.*

****

Later that night… Janey, are you still counting? I cannot believe you counted all those envelopes tonight; so many people gave money and gifts. Did you make a list of who gave what?
Yes, Bobby. You know I did. You saw me writing, didn't you, Janey said in a playful tone! I know who gave what and how much we received from each attendee. Some people gave a gift and money. We made out great! We have a nice cushion to get started with.
Cool, how much money was inside the card box? Now I'm curious.
I counted $6,890, give or take a dollar or two, I'm a little sleepy and maybe partially tipsy. I'll recount in the morning.
Oh, wow, yeah; we made out pretty good, Babe, that's great!
Bobby, I was thinking; we should put the money in a saving account and use it for a down payment on a house, as opposed to renting. Let's be patient and become homeowners.

Bobby pauses… Janey, you are so savvy, you truly are my match… I was going to wait until we came back from our honeymoon, but I purchased *us* a house in Mumford Heights two weeks ago—it's exactly what you said you always wanted. It has hardwood floors, a sunroom, patio, walk-in closet, a finished basement, and a wood-burning fireplace, plus so much more…

Mumford "88"

You did what? You purchased us a house? How, when, why? Oh, my goodness, I cannot believe it, I cannot wait to see it… Wow, a house of my own!

Your reaction is priceless and means the world to me; that smile makes my heart beat faster. As for the house, you will see it in due time. And you are correct, renting is a no-no, especially if we don't have to. You know I'm going to take care of you, we are married—and we have noisy ass sex, you know how loud you get. Besides, living with our parents isn't a good start. And you are correct, the financial gifts we received from the wedding guest can be used to help with the closing cost and down payment for the house; we settle in three weeks. I borrowed a few thousand dollars from my father—even though he keeps insisting that I don't have to pay him back. I took your mom to see the house, Janey, and she loves it. Honestly, I didn't think your mom could keep the secret, but she did.

So, is it fair to say that I'm a wife—and, in a few weeks, we are going to become homeowners? Yes, Janey, it is fair to say all the above. And don't forget to mention, you're a college graduate with a degree in psychology—and a future Olympic track star, I lucked out, babe.

We both are lucked to have found each other. God is good. I'm quoting my college roommate Sarah when I say, "when we do our part, the universe abides."

Yes, Janey, words so true, I agree completely. Nothing works out in anyone's favor unless we do our part to succeed. With that being said, know that I will adore you always—and we will have a prosperous life—despite trials and tribulations because nothing in life is easy, including marriage. As long as our love is sincere, we will withstand the test of time. I will do my part as your husband, and I know you will do your part as my wife. As long as we both work to make our marriage work, it shall.

Yes, Bobby, I will do my part to keep our marriage strong, and I will love you even when I'm upset with you, you have my word. I love you so much, and I'm so happy to be your wife. You have truly made me the happiest woman in the world—and the house, what a bonus! Can we make a toast, can we toast to our marriage and the new home?

Sure, Janey. I'll toast to that. Besides, a toast gives me another reason to kiss your scrumptious lips… *Bobby kisses Janey subtly on the lips; then, they sip on champagne as they cherish the moment.*

****

Even later that night… Now that our wedding day has come and gone and we are settled in for the evening… Mrs. Hall, get your fine ass over here and make love to your husband. I've been craving you all night long. I love your vajayjay, babe; it's so fucking good. And I know you're craving this dick. The way you sucked it earlier expressed how much you love it…

Yup, you know I love that vanilla dick; it's always so hard and solid. The perfect fit for my puzzle—I mean pussy. Now fuck me and show me how much you want this pussy…

You don't have to ask me twice. Look down, see my soldier pointing at you? He's at full salute; the eye is looking right at you and is ready to go in, literally. I can't wait to cumin in you, babe. *Janey's breathing intensifies*, enough with the flirty fore-play talk, put your thick-hard dick inside of me. Make me feel amazing; make me cum all over your dick. Give me your hand, feel me; I'm so fucking wet right now. *Sacred energy exchange is in full force.*

Damn girl, you are wet, fuck. But first, I want to caress your pussy with my tongue; I love how that pussy taste when it's wet and juicy like this, *Janey moans with anticipation… Bobby says no more, he turns down the lights in the room and caresses his wife's entire body with his tongue and breath. He blows on her body ever so softly. Janey moans with pleasure, then Bobby slowly goes down between her legs and says, I'm ready to eat your chocolate cookie; his breath stimulates her vagina… Do you want to feel my tongue on your clitoris? He's teasing her…. and Janey is so aroused, she orgasms… the thought alone took her over the edge… Bobby continues to caress his wife's body as he performs oral sex on her, and within five minutes, Janey orgasms again. Bobby says, your extremely aroused tonight, then he proceeds to insert his penis into her vagina… And when he does, Janey's body goes crazy as she moans with intense pleasure,* oh my, oh shit, ohooohoh, oh god, owww, fuck I'm cuming… he had her speaking in tongues.

Damn babe, I've never felt you this stimulated before… I'm not going to last much longer—it's too warm and slippery… *The moment was intense; Sacred energy exchange was off the charts... It was an electrifying experience, the sounds of Janey moans, the way her pussy pulsated on his penis, the way she wrapped her legs around his body, the way she rubbed and squeezed his ass—made him orgasm within minutes… Bobby and Janey laid there in pure ecstasy... they both knew round two was underway, they won't be getting much sleep tonight. The happy couple made love several times throughout the night and took showers between lovemaking. And when morning* came, Bobby had a morning hardon; thus, Janey woke Bobby with a blowjob. Janey loved the way his warm secretions exploded into her mouth, though she couldn't swallow, she enjoyed the symbolism of his cum dripping from her mouth. Hello, married life they both proclaimed. Sex with no limits... Bobby wanted to have sex in the late morning, but Janey's vagina was sore; thus, she told him he had to wait until tonight—after she took a hot, relaxing bubble bath. Of course, Bobby couldn't wait to join her.

After their sexcapades, they made a few calls then got dressed for the day; they celebrated their first day as husband and wife at local venues, and they had dinner at a fancy restaurant. They both felt happy and content with their life and was looking forward to their future together. Two days later, they traveled to Hawaii for their honeymoon, and they made the best of every day. They even participated in an "A luau" (Hawaiian feast); here is where they meet Todd and Mona, who would later become near and dear friends of theirs... They basked in the Hawaiian sun and, at the same time, was looking forward to returning home and spending the rest of their life together. Indeed, it was a life to look forward too.

Chapter 23: Conclusion

And like the true friend that Janey is, she kept her word to Tray's memory, and she qualified for a spot in the 1996 Summer Olympics—she went on to win a silver medal in the 200-meter run. In addition, Janey set a record for the 100-meter run; she was the youngest female to achieve such an accomplishment. And with top-speed, Janey reached goals she never imagined. Janey retired her running shoes after winning a gold medal, which is the highest achievement in the sport. Janey used her popularity and earnings to open a successful Clothing Boutique and a Mindfulness Center. The Mindfulness Center specialized in helping people find their happiness, their way. Her philosophy is, "It all starts from within; the power to change your life is found within oneself." Janey always tells people, "You and you alone hold the power," she encourages people to look deeper into oneself to find the answers... Janey also specialized in helping children cope with childhood drama, rape, violence, etc. Ms. Ava often volunteers at Janey's businesses and became a peer counselor to parents who lost their children to illness and/or violent crimes. Janey wanted to employ Ava, but Ava wouldn't dream of taking payment from Janey. Janey set up a tip bowel—which inspired customers to give Ava love offerings.

Mumford "88"

Bobby often worked with his wife, and he became a positive impact in his community via positive policing. In fact, he started the "positive policing" slogan, which swiftly spread to other police departments. Bobby worked as a full-time officer for a little over ten years before he decided to work fulltime with his wife. Putting people behind bars was no longer his career choice; however, he stayed employed as a part-time cop so that he wouldn't lose his pension... Bobby focused on helping people turn their lives around; hence, keeping them out of jail. He helped men become better fathers, husbands, sons, brothers, etc. Bobby was an influential role model, and he mentored heaps of men in his community and neighboring areas.

Janey and Bobby eventually opened two other Mindfulness Centers and Counseling Agencies throughout the Tri-states; they were a successful and happy couple. They kept their morals and values at high standards—and the universe rewarded them generously.

Janey and Bobby had their first child on their 11th wedding anniversary. They decided to hold off on having children right away. They wanted to establish their careers and, most importantly, help others succeed in life. They named their daughter Navaya Bobbie Hall and their son Jonas Bobby Hall.

Bobby and Janey's relationship is built on honesty and love; thus, it has a solid foundation. Happy to say the spirited and selfless couple helped many families find their path to freedom, liberty, and happiness. Janey and Bobby live happily ever after.

The End

Amazon.com/author/vanessabellejackson77

DOASM77@gmail.com

Facebook: Doasm Memoir

Instagram: Nurse_belle77

https://www.facebook.com/doasm.book.5

Mumford "88"

Note to self: *Soul Mate:* What is needed to find your soul mate? Indeed, some people are not meant to be in long-term relationships, ensure you do not fall for those spirits. Heartache and sorrow will follow.

"Two signs of not knowing your worth: You settle for less—and tolerate conditions you're not comfortable with" (original author unknown). Do not settle—know your worth.

Guided Mindfulness Scripts

Mindfulness is being aware of our thoughts and feelings (without Judgement) – when mindful, we are aware of the way a person, situation, or experience makes us feel. Mindfulness is a way to train the mind; thus, reducing stressors in life. Simply being aware can aid in a happier life.

Awareness of Feelings: Sitting or lying in a comfortable position, take a deep breath in then exhale your day away. Focus on the *now*, bringing your attention to your mind & body—notice how you're feeling within your body at this very moment. Take note of the feeling, and remember it's only a feeling, don't let it be more than what it is.

If possible, allow your body to relax as you scan your emotions—let your shoulders ease downward if you are sitting – or allow your body to melt into your yoga mate if you're lying flat. Feel the day melt away as you focus on the *now*. Use the next few minutes to unwind—close your eyes and meditate—allowing the energy of the moment to lead your thoughts, feelings, and emotions.

Relaxation Techniques: Discovering ways to calm and relax the mind and body during stressful times and situations is priceless... Please find a comfortable position—the goal is to breathe through difficulties, thus reducing stress and tension that may lie silently in the body. Take a deep breath in to nourish your body and mind with oxygen, oh, the power of air—an essential element that keeps our bodies going. When we breathe in, envision oneself inhaling positive thoughts, feelings, needs, wants, etc., into our bodies. Breathing in what we want—

and exhaling what we do not. As we exhale, we breathe out negative thoughts, emotions, feelings, energies, etc., that may be hiding within our bodies—for negativity is not wanted here; thus, we create ways to release them.

Focusing Techniques: Maybe you can focus on your physical body, do you notice any tension that is built up, or maybe you notice your body feels at ease? Whatever the case may be, take notice and become aware of what you are feeling. What thoughts or emotions developed? Make a note of it and move on, again, without judgment.

Maybe your mind has a lot of mental chatter at the moment; that too is okay, let the thoughts be what they are, (thoughts) and find an anchor to bring you back to the present moment. An anchor could be your breath, white noise, meditation music, even something you hold in your hand, the choice is *always* yours.

Maybe you're focusing on the symphony of your environment—the birds chirping, the horn that is beeping outside, the noise that you hear from the other room, your brother or sister playing, the rain falling, etc., Listen, without judgment.

Maybe you can take a few moments to sit in silence—discovering inner peace within yourself—a mental vacation from the outside world. This moment is about you, finding ways to discover you. If possible, relax for a few more minutes before completing this exercise. How do you feel after sitting in silence? **There can be power in silence. Namaste.**

Mumford "88"

Note to Self:

Mumford "88"

Note to Self:

Mumford "88"

Note to Self:

Mumford "88"

Note to Self:

Mumford "88"

Blurb

Extra, Extra, read all about it. "Mumford 88" is an erotic and exciting short story filled with murder and suspense. Tray is an athletic teenager who is keeping an awful secret from her mother and best friend. All Tray wants to do is complete her senior year of high school so she can go to college and live in peace. But the issue with secrets is they have a way of biting people in the ass. Read how one person's secret could lead to a life of pain and regrets. And how a best friend's determination to right a wrong—changes her life in ways she could have never imagined.

Made in the USA
Columbia, SC
01 May 2020